LOVING TESSA

RACHEL HANNA

PROLOGUE

*A*aron Parker sat on the edge of the dock and cast his fishing line back into the still waters of the north Georgia mountain lake. He was thankful that one of his oldest friends from high school in January Cove had loaned him his cabin for a week so that he could get some rest and attempt to forget what his life had become in the last several months. But the fish weren't biting, and he was growing frustrated instead of relaxed.

The quiet of the mountains was very different from what he was used to in January Cove. He didn't realize how loud those crashing ocean waves could be until he sat on the edge of that dock and surveyed the still waters of the small lake. Simplicity. That's what he needed right now. The ocean was too complicated, brought back too many memories of the life that was taken from him.

He'd met Natalie Jenkins three and half years ago at a New Year's party with friends. They'd had an immediate attraction, but who wouldn't have been attracted to Natalie? She was stunning with her long blond hair and sparkling green eyes that shot right through his soul. He'd known from the first moment he'd laid eyes on her that she was "the one". He could see them sitting on their front porch overlooking the ocean in January Cove with a passel of kids running around. He could see them as old people walking down the beach, hand in hand.

But apparently, Natalie saw something else.

After dating for three years, he'd popped the question on New Year's Eve as a reminder of when they had met. She'd excitedly said yes, and they began planning the wedding of her dreams. They would marry on the beach, of course, and honeymoon in Hawaii. Aaron had never been happier, but maybe that was how he missed the signs.

She'd started working later and later. She'd started going out with her girlfriends for drinks. She wasn't looking for her wedding dress yet, even though most women would have been scouring the surrounding areas for the perfect gown. Not Natalie. She'd changed very soon after accepting his proposal. She wouldn't set a date, said she was so busy with work.

She was a marketing executive at a small advertising agency, so it didn't make sense to him that she was staying late at work or delaying their wedding. Her hours were nine to five, and he couldn't think of any valid reason that she'd be staying late over and over. He wanted to ignore his gut feelings, but he couldn't. He knew enough to know that something was going on, and he couldn't stake the rest of his life on a woman who might be up to no good.

So, one evening when she said she was working late, he followed her. Even though it made him feel completely stalker-ish, he had to know what was going on. So, he rented a car, put on a baseball cap and waited outside of her work. As she left, he noticed a man walking with her. They seemed awfully friendly for co-workers, and she was doing "the laugh". He recognized that laugh as her way of flirting, and his stomach churned.

After driving over to Savannah, they got out at a bed & breakfast where she and Aaron had stayed on several occasions. Nausea overwhelmed him as he watched them walk inside, holding hands the whole way.

Aaron followed them inside and waited for the front desk lady to appear. She was an old friend of his, and when he entered her face went white.

"Aaron," she said softly.

"Hi, Joanna," he said pursing his lips. "I think you know why I'm here."

"I do. And I'm so sorry..."

"I need the key, Joanna." Her eyes went wide, and she shook her head no.

"Aaron, you know I can't give you the key." A shy and sweet Southern woman, Joanna Eldridge was the epitome of a wallflower. But, she was kind hearted and everyone liked her.

"Joanna, I need to see for myself."

"I can't have you here fighting with some guy."

"I won't. I promise. I'm here to let her know that we're done. That's it. No fighting or yelling or causing a scene. I swear to you."

She stood silently for a moment before sliding the key across the front desk. "I have to take care of something in the back. But, I cannot and will not give you a key, Aaron," she said with a sly smile as she left the key sitting in plain sight. He took a deep breath as she walked away and then retrieved the key from the desk.

As he walked up the hallway to room six, he knew that his life was about to change forever. Everything he'd thought was in his future was now gone, and it was about to be replaced by something he would have never imagined.

He quietly inserted the key in the door, but then he realized that it was still unlocked. He turned the knob and opened the door to see Natalie climbing onto the bed in sexy lingerie that he'd purchased for her on Valentine's Day. She was supposed to wear it on their honeymoon. The guy was already in bed, completely naked and waiting for Aaron's fiancee.

"What the..." the guy shouted, causing Natalie to turn around and see Aaron standing there, frozen in place with his anger building.

Natalie looked like a deer caught in headlights and tried to cover herself with a blanket from the foot of the bed. Aaron found that odd given that he'd seen every part of her. Why would she cover up for him? He noticed the sparkle of her engagement ring shining from the dresser.

"Who the hell are you?" the guy said as he stood up

and put another blanket around his waist. He was about Aaron's size, and Aaron had fought enough with his brothers growing up to know that he could probably take him, but he'd promised Joanna that he wouldn't make a scene. Instead, he took in a sharp breath and looked back at Natalie who had tears already running down her cheeks.

"Roger, don't..." she said grabbing his arm as he stalked toward Aaron. "He's my fiancé."

"Your fiancé?"

"Didn't you notice that big, shiny ring on her finger, jackass?" Aaron asked through gritted teeth.

"Aaron!" Natalie chided, which astonished him. What right did she have to react to anything he said to her lover?

"Look, man, I had no idea she was engaged." The guy put both of his hands up and smiled as he shook his head. "She's a fun time, but I don't make a habit of breaking up relationships." Natalie looked at him with her eyes wide and her mouth hanging open.

"Really?" Aaron said rolling his eyes. "Well, here's the good news, buddy. She's not engaged anymore," he said as he snatched the ring off the dresser and turned to walk out the door.

"Wait! Aaron!" she yelled behind him as she grabbed her robe and followed him into the hall, tugging at the tie to get it closed. "Aaron, please!" she said loudly. He stopped, but he didn't turn around. The thought of looking at her made him feel sick.

"Natalie, we have nothing to talk about. There is not

one thing you could say that would change anything here. It's over."

"Aaron, I was just scared and stressed. The pressure of the wedding..."

Aaron turned around swiftly and glared into her eyes. Those eyes that used to mean everything to him now looked hollow. "Don't you dare blame this on the wedding. I proposed to you because I wanted to spend the rest of my life with you, Nat. I wanted to have children with you, wake up every morning with my arms around you, grow old with you. I offered you everything I have, and I never betrayed you. And for what? So I could walk in while you were hooking up with some guy from your office?"

"How did you know he was from my office?" she asked, a hint of anger in her voice. "Wait. Did you follow me here?" Her anger was palpable, and he couldn't imagine how she thought she had the right to be mad at all.

"What does it matter?"

"You invaded my privacy. That's like... stalking!" she said sharply.

"You can't be serious," Aaron said running his fingers through his blond hair and sighing. "Well, don't worry, because I won't follow you anywhere ever again. As far as I'm concerned, you don't exist."

With that, Aaron turned and walked down the hall. He dropped the key on the desk as he left, wishing that he never had to think about Natalie again but knowing it was impossible.

Of course, it wasn't the last he heard from her

either. She'd continued calling him and showing up at the campground for a couple of weeks after he caught her. She never really asked to get back together; instead, she had tried to prove that it was the first and only time she had cheated on him for some reason. He never really understood the point of talking about it all, but she had always been a bit of a "right fighter". She really just wanted to prove to herself that she wasn't a bad person, but Aaron was angry. He was much angrier than he'd thought he could ever get at her or any woman.

His heart had been broken - no, shattered - into a million pieces. At twenty-seven years old, he knew that swearing off women forever wasn't realistic, but for now he had no interest. How could he ever trust another woman again?

As he cast his fishing line back into the water, he breathed in the clean mountain air trying to wash away the thoughts that seemed to be embedded in his mind forever. He didn't like the way that she still had a hold over him, even though she had moved on long ago. It had only been four months since their breakup, but he'd seen her around town with various men in recent weeks, and it made him wonder about his own ability to choose a good woman. How hadn't he seen her flaws before?

If he was honest with himself, he wanted what his brother Kyle had with Jenna. Even after all those years apart, they had managed to find their way back to each other a few weeks ago. It was like fate or God stepped in and pulled them back to where they needed to be, and Aaron wished he was that lucky. When it came to love and finding a life partner, he was starting over from scratch and it didn't feel good. While his best friends from January Cove were all married and had families of their own, he was sitting on a dock alone wishing that his former fiancee hadn't been such a cheater.

Anger boiling through his veins again, he slammed his fishing pole down on the dock and watched it break into two pieces. He put his head in his hands and growled as he realized that this little mountain trip wasn't alleviating his stress any more than being back home in January Cove. Natalie followed him wherever he went because she was firmly implanted in his mind. At that moment, he decided that it was time to go back home after just five days in the mountains because at least he could occupy his mind with work rather than sitting around alone thinking about her.

CHAPTER 1

It was quiet. Maybe too quiet. Tessa Reeves stared out the window of her small camper, looking at the ocean that came in and out like clockwork. Just like the breath going in and out of her lungs without effort and thought, the ocean rolled in and out all day long. The sound of it both calmed and terrified her, but she had to put the terrifying thoughts out of her mind. Otherwise, she might roll into a ball on the floor and implode.

Her camper wasn't much, but it was all she was able to afford. Saving up her money for months, she was glad to have been able to purchase it at all. It was old, but it ran, and that was all that counted at the moment. It got her to where she needed to go, and it was her protection right now.

Nestled under a tree at the Crystal Cove campground, she felt safe, but she knew better than anyone that safety was only an illusion and could be taken away at any moment. She wasn't going to let her guard down for anyone, so she'd been keeping to herself inside the small camper with her dog, Beau, and her three year old, Tyler.

It wasn't easy to keep a dog and a toddler occupied inside of a small camper all day every day, but it was what she had to do right now until there was a better plan. She prayed that there would be a better plan soon, although she couldn't imagine a scenario that would keep her and Tyler safe.

For the last four days, she had stared out at the ocean waves, willing them to take her fears and anxieties away. So far she wasn't having much luck. For the first time in six years, she was on her own in the world. It was both scary and liberating, thrilling and terrifying.

Tyler was taking a nap, so she took the opportunity to start preparations for dinner. Money was tight, and she couldn't spare much. Getting a job would have been great, but she couldn't take the risk of being seen in public or leaving Tyler alone, so she'd have to get by as long as possible on the small amount of groceries she'd brought with her and the little bit of money she had tucked away under the flattened mattress of her bed in the back of the camper.

For awhile, she had been used to a bigger space, a nice sized house on the beach with a big kitchen and a spacious master bedroom. But she felt freer in her current space than she ever had in her old home, so she wasn't going to complain. Plus, that luxurious facade of a life had been short lived anyway. She hadn't seen the beach up close in years.

She was less than two hours from her former life, but right now it felt a world away. She'd had to make a choice, and now she had to deal with the consequences of doing that.

An evening storm rolled over the ocean, and she stared out the tiny window of her camper as she hand washed the few dishes she'd brought along. As the thunder rumbled and the rain started to come down, she wondered how she was going to do this. How would she raise a little boy on the run?

~

AARON DROVE through the pounding rain, typical for this time of year at the beach, and finally pulled into his driveway. After hours on the road, he was glad to be back home in January Cove. It wasn't that he didn't appreciate what his friend had done by letting him use the mountain cabin, but relaxation wasn't working for him right now. He needed to busy his mind. Too much space in his thoughts only led to thinking about Natalie, about the life he thought he was going to have but wouldn't.

He lived in a small cabin at the campground, opting to stay in total control of what was going on there at any given time. He'd been running the campground for three years, and in that time he had grown it well. Adding a restaurant had allowed the campground to bring in more money, and he was almost done with renovations to the small mini golf course that visiting kids loved the most.

With over one hundred RV sites, there were always a lot of visitors during this time of the year. Summer was the busy season in the hot and humid coastal town, and Aaron made it his job to know each of his guests and ensure they were having a good time.

Most of the camp sites had grills, tables and other hookups for the RV visitors. It also had bath houses, a laundromat for those who didn't have a washer and dryer in their campers, a boat dock and a small store where visitors could stock up on essentials.

For the kids, Crystal Cove had an arcade and game room, fishing and even paddle boats. Of course, there was a swimming pool, playground and a place to play horseshoes. The idea was for everyone to enjoy their stay so they would always come back and visit.

Aaron loved the constant chaos of running such a bustling campground. It kept his mind occupied, especially during the busy season. While others might need to sit quietly to relax, working was his form of relaxation. His hope was that one day the business in his mind would finally push Natalie out of there for good. Until then, he'd run his business and put up that mental barricade himself.

He pulled into the cabin, which was adjacent to some of the smaller RV spaces at the campground, and held a duffel bag over his head for protection from the pounding rain as he yanked on his bigger suitcase in the back of the SUV. Suddenly, without warning, a big dog jumped up behind him and pushed against his legs causing him to collide with the back of the SUV.

Grasping at the tailgate, he caught himself before hitting the pavement.

"Dang it!" he yelled over the rain as he watched his bags fall to the ground in a heap. The dog, a boxer it seemed, continued to jump up as it excitedly licked him in the face and barked.

"I'm so sorry!" He heard a woman's frantic voice behind him and watched as she attached a leash to her unruly dog and pulled him back. Reaching out a hand, she attempted to offer assistance to Aaron as he ambled up from the ground. He didn't take her hand, and he barely looked at her at first. "He slipped out the door. I'm so sorry," she said. For the first time, he looked at her. Her brown hair was soaking wet and sticking to her face. With her tanned skin and crystal clear blue eyes, she was a beautiful woman but there was a hint of fear - or was it sadness - in her voice and in her eyes.

"It's okay. You'd better get back inside with him, though. This storm seems to be really kicking up."

"At least let me help you get your stuff inside. I can put him up..."

"No, really. It's okay. Save yourself," Aaron said with a laugh as he pointed back at her camper. She returned his smile, although timidly, and then turned back to the small camper.

Aaron stood in the rain for a moment, no longer caring about the droplets pounding on his head, and wondered about the beautiful, wet woman in the small, dilapidated camper next to his house. One thing was for sure - he would find out more about her as soon as he possibly could.

~

"CRAP!" she yelled as soon as she was back inside of her camper. "Beau! Bad boy!" she snapped at the dog. He hung his head and slid behind a chair.

So much for her goal of not letting anyone see her. Hopefully she hadn't done too much damage by showing her face to the mystery man that Beau had befriended in the rain. Maybe he wouldn't remember her face, after all she was drenching wet when he saw her.

She looked down at her clothes that were now clinging to her and decided that she'd better change them so she didn't get sick. The last thing she needed was to have to go to the local doctor or hospital.

As she peeled her dripping wet clothes off, she thought about the interaction with the handsome stranger. Who was he? Obviously, he was staying in the cute little cabin next to her lot, and he was one of the sexiest men she'd ever laid two eyes on.

"Stop thinking like that, Tessa," she chided to herself. She was in no position to have those kind of thoughts about any man. Her life was in enough upheaval without involving a man in it.

"Mommy?" Tyler called as he ran across the small living area.

"I'm changing my clothes, honey," she said from behind the door of the tiny bathroom.

"I'm hungry," he moaned. She felt like the world's worst mother. Her son was hungry, and she'd all but forgotten to make dinner.

"I'll make you something in just a minute, sweetie," she said, trying not to show the stress in her voice. Tyler didn't need any more stress. His short life had been full of it.

Tessa dug a can of ravioli out of a box that she'd brought along for her trip and opened it up. While Tyler was wolfing it down a few minutes later, she took out a towel and attempted to dry Beau off and clean the water droplets all over the floor. This camper was her refuge, and she had to make sure that she took care of it.

~

"MORNING, BOSS," Paul Gallagher said in his normal cheerful tone. Paul had been working for Aaron for about a year, doing all kinds of odd jobs around the campground. He also ran the register at their small store most of the time.

"Good morning," Aaron said as he absent mindedly looked through receipts that had accumulated in the five days he was gone.

"You're back early. How was the trip?"

"Boring."

"Wasn't that the point? To get some quiet time away from the chaos here?"

"Didn't work," Aaron said still not looking up. If there was one thing he'd learned in his life, it was that his blue eyes always gave him away. It was better to hide them by looking down. "So, update me on what's been going on around here since I left."

15

"The Morgan family finally left," Paul said holding his hands up to the sky as if he was thanking God for that fact.

"Thank goodness. They were such a pain. Who stays at a tourist RV park for six weeks anyway?"

"And who has ten kids packed into an RV?" Paul said shaking his head. "Those were some of the worst kids we've ever had here."

"What else did I miss?"

"We got a new woman here about four days ago. She's next to your cabin."

"Yeah, I met her dog last night," Aaron said through gritted teeth. "She came out in the rain and got him."

"I only met her briefly when she checked in. Her name is Dawn, I think."

"Dawn," Aaron repeated without thinking. "She doesn't look like a Dawn." The comment was odd, even to Aaron himself.

"She keeps to herself. In fact, I haven't seen her come out since she got here."

"Why would you rent a space at the beach and then stay in your camper?" Aaron asked.

"Don't know. We might want to watch her, though." Aaron knew what Paul was referring to. They'd had a fugitive stay at the park one time. He'd killed his girl-friend near Atlanta and used the park to hide out from the police for almost two weeks before they located him.

"Well, I'm in a great position to do that since I'm right next door," Aaron said.

"Maybe she's just trying to get some quiet time,

unlike some people I know," Paul joked. Aaron didn't laugh, but grumbled instead as he went back to looking at receipts. Paul knew enough about him to know that it was best to leave well enough alone when Aaron was in a bad mood.

As Paul walked out, Aaron realized that his mind still wasn't relaxed enough to look through the receipts, so he decided to take a walk on the property. There was always something to do at the campground, and he liked to fiddle around looking for the next project or repair.

He walked outside, glancing first at the mystery woman's camper to see if she was outside. No such luck. He wondered for a moment if Paul was right. Could she be some kind of fugitive? She sure didn't look dangerous. With her voluptuous curves showing themselves through her wet, clingy clothing, she looked like a woman he could definitely snuggle up to at night. Shooing the thought away, Aaron groaned as he made his way up the path closest to the store.

CHAPTER 2

"So, those are the numbers for the quarter so far," Aaron said as he slid the papers across the table to his mother. Adele Parker, the town's most revered business woman and mother to five kids, smiled at her son as she slid her glasses down her nose.

"Sweetie, you don't have to sound so business-like with me. I'm your momma," she said with a chuckle.

"I'm well aware of that, Mom, but this is our business." As soon as the words had escaped his mouth, he regretted them. They'd feared they would lose her to the mild stroke she'd had recently, and the last thing he wanted to do was make her feel bad. "Sorry. It's been a rough few weeks. I'm still not myself, I guess." He reached across the table and patted her hand.

"I understand, baby. When you lose the one you thought you'd spend the rest of your life with, it rocks your entire world. Don't rush things. All I ask as your mother is that you don't close your heart off to those who love you."

"I promise. So, how are you feeling?"

"Good. Now that I have Jenna here helping me, things are working much better. She's a smart cookie, that one."

"I'm glad she and Kyle found their way back to each other," Aaron said forcing a smile. He was happy for his brother, but he couldn't help but be a little jealous at the same time.

Aaron finished up his meeting with Adele and then headed back to the campground. As he pulled in, he could see the mystery woman behind her camper wrestling with her dog. She looked like she was losing, and Aaron parked just in time to see the big dog standing over her on the ground.

"Come here, buddy!" he yelled in an attempt to get him off of her. The dog ran straight toward him, and Aaron grabbed him by the collar. As he did, the woman timidly made her way toward him. She seemed almost scared to come closer to him. "You okay?" Aaron asked looking up as he held onto the dog.

"Me? Um, sure. I was just giving him a bath..."

"With all due respect, it looked more like he was about to maul you."

"Beau wouldn't hurt me. He's my buddy," she said smiling as she reached out and rubbed the dog. "He just got too excited."

"If you say so," Aaron said standing up. The woman quickly clipped the dog into the leash. "Aaron Parker. I own this place." He reached out to shake her hand, but she stared down at her feet.

"Nice to meet you," she said without looking up. "I better go." She started to walk back to the camper.

"And you are?" he called to her.

"You own this place, so I am sure you know my name," she said as she turned around and smiled. Her dark hair had a shine under the sunlight streaming through the tall trees surrounding the campground, and the curve of her neck sent chills up his spine. She had a natural, rare beauty unlike the women he saw walking up and down the beach everyday in their often too-tight bikinis and fake tans.

"Remind me," Aaron said with a smile. She was starting to both arouse and irritate him.

"Dana," she said as she walked into the camper and shut the door. Dana?

~

"AND YOU'RE sure she said Dawn?" Aaron asked Paul from across the counter.

"Positive. See? Here's her paperwork," Paul said sliding it across the countertop.

Aaron stared at it for a moment and then sighed as he slapped it back down onto the hard surface. "Why is this lady lying?"

"Maybe you should ask her."

"But she hasn't done anything wrong while she's been staying here, so don't you think it would be a little odd for me to ask her? I mean, there's no law against using a fake name. She paid cash, right?"

"Yep. She paid cash in advance for three weeks.

After that, I have no idea where she will go or if she'll pay more to stay here."

Aaron ran his fingers through his hair, a common stressed out trait of the Parker men. As he thought through his options, he realized that he couldn't just go and confront a woman for not being overly friendly. Maybe she didn't want people to know her real name out of an abundance of caution for some reason. Either way, he had enough to deal with in his own life, so he opted to leave her alone for the time being.

"So, have you heard from Natalie lately?" Paul asked. Just the sound of her name crossing someone's lips made Aaron sick to his stomach.

"No, and I don't want to. Don't mention her name again, okay?" Aaron said pointedly as he looked into Paul's eyes. Paul swallowed hard.

"Sorry. Just making conversation."

"Well, she's no longer a topic of conversations that include me. Understand?"

"Yes, sir," Paul said as he watched his boss's face finally relax.

"I've gotta run. I need to check on some things around the beach area," he said as he slipped his sunglasses onto his face and walked out the door.

～

TESSA WIPED THE TINY COUNTER, cleaning up random bits of tomato sauce from her attempt at making a decent meal of spaghetti. She feared that her son would never know what good food tasted like as she wasn't the best cook in the world, and when she wasn't damaging his taste buds with her own cooking, he was eating from a can or a jar.

"Mommy? Go to the beach?" Tyler said with his pleading blue eyes. He'd been asking for days now. It had been impossible to keep him from seeing the ocean waves out of the tiny camper windows.

"Not today, sweetie," she said patting the tuft of blond hair on his head. It was the same hair his father had. The same head of hair she'd fallen in love with and subsequently come to fear. Maybe Tyler's hair would darken as he got older. She hoped so, and that made her feel guilty for wanting anything about her son to change.

"Why not?" he asked with tears welling in his eyes. How could she tell him that they were in hiding? How could she explain that it wasn't worth the risk to go outside more than they had to, even though they were hours from home.

"Honey, it's getting late. It's after dinner. We need to get baths…" she said. He started to cry. She knew this was hard for him. He'd been uprooted from everything he knew, even if what he knew was violence. His toys were gone. His room was gone. Guilt rose like bile in her throat, and she turned away from him to stop her own tears from escaping.

The truth was that she couldn't give Tyler a real bath anymore. The old vintage camper had a small stand-up shower with a handheld hose. When she bathed her son, it felt like she was giving her dog a bath. What kind of mother was she? Every option she'd weighed hadn't seemed safe. The only way to be safe was to be alone. She'd learned that the hard way. But Tyler was now paying the price for her poor decisions from long ago.

As Tessa looked outside, she saw the sun starting to set over the ocean. Maybe they could sneak down to the shore and Tyler could play in the ocean for a little while without anyone noticing. Most people would be near their motorhomes and camp sites getting dinner ready. Deciding that it was worth the risk, she turned to Tyler.

"Okay, bud, I've got a surprise for you!" she said smiling as Tyler's eyes got bigger. "We're going to put on our swimsuits and play in the ocean for a little bit before it gets too dark."

Tyler squealed with delight as he jumped up and down. Within minutes, he was buck naked running to the tiny bedroom on the other end of the camper, throwing the few articles of clothing in his rolling suitcase up in the air. Tessa giggled as she watched him. It was the first bit of normalcy she'd felt in a long time, and she prayed that showing their faces on the beach wouldn't prove to be a big mistake.

∽

AARON SAT on the small front porch of his cabin with a beer in one hand and his cell phone in the other. He wasn't expecting a call, but it was a habit of his to keep his phone close ever since his mother's stroke. Plus, running a campground meant that anything could happen at any minute, so he liked to be reachable.

As he swigged a sip of his beer, he leaned back in his chair and surveyed the beautiful sunset view. He couldn't help but look at the old camper next to his cabin and wonder where the beautiful, if not secretive, woman and her unruly dog were. Were they inside, cooped up like convicts? Or had they finally gone somewhere. It seemed awfully quiet over there.

Tired of sitting still, he got up and walked toward the beach, dropping his bottle of beer into one of many receptacles along the way. The last thing he wanted was for any of his patrons to see him chugging alcohol as he walked around the campground. Most of his customers seemed to be near their campers, firing up their grills for dinner time.

What he saw next stopped him in his tracks. It was her. She was wearing a pale pink two piece bathing suit, and the orange glow of the sunset radiated off her skin even from far away. The gentle sea breeze was lightly blowing her long hair across her shoulders, and she seemed relaxed for the first time since he'd seen her. As she ran her fingers through her hair and stared into the ocean, he couldn't help but feel like she was haunted by something. Or maybe someone.

As he moved closer, he crouched behind a dune. Feeling a bit like a stalker again, he decided that he needed to at least know what was up with this reclusive woman staying on his property. Suddenly, he heard a child's voice screaming and crying, and she began to run toward the outcropping of jagged rocks near the shore. He froze in place for a moment as he saw her, panic-stricken, running across the sand toward the sound of a small child crying.

Without thinking, he ran from behind the dune to find her crouched next to a rock and scooping a small boy up into her arms. She clutched him close to her, and Aaron's legs felt like they were in quick sand as everything seemed to go in slow motion. He knew he was running, but he couldn't get to her or the child fast enough for his taste. What was that about?

With no time to think too hard, he called out to her. "Is he okay?"

"I don't know!" she said through tears as she looked back at him with a terrified look in her eyes. Aaron finally made it to her and fell to his knees beside her. There was a big cut across the boy's forehead, but at least he was crying. Still, the mound forming behind the cut was threatening to open it up even larger.

"We need to get him over to the urgent care center," Aaron yelled above the sound of the waves crashing against the adjacent rocks. "Come on!" he yelled as he stood up. He carefully took the small boy into his arms and she stood up beside him. They ran toward his cabin with the boy crying all the way. As they reached his cabin, he unlocked the Jeep with his remote and carefully placed the boy in the back seat, buckling him in and trying to assure him everything was going to be alright.

"It's going to be okay, Tyler," she said, trying to soothe him through her own tears as she sat close to him in the backseat. "Thank you for taking us. My camper... it doesn't really..." she said pointing to the beaten up old clunker that she and her son were living in.

"It's okay. Glad to do it. Doc Clayton is the best around here, and he's usually working at the urgent care center today. They stay open pretty late, so he should still be there."

"Okay..." she said, obviously tending to Tyler and paying little attention to Aaron. Still, as he drove, he couldn't help but listen to her genuine love for the little boy. The sounds of a real mother, much like his own. It took him back in time to those days when his mother was the only parent around to soothe him. Every skinned knee, broken bone, broken heart. His father was gone before he ever had a chance to know him. Where was this little boy's father?

Within a few minutes, Aaron was pulling into the parking lot of the urgent care center. Before he had a chance, she swooped the boy out of the car and inside like she had the strength of ten men. There was just something about the protection of a mother. It left him in awe for a moment as he watched her push the double doors open before he had a chance to open them for her like the Southern gentleman he'd been brought up to be.

"Can I help you?" the woman behind the counter asked.

"Can't you see? He has a cut on his head and this bump is forming..." she stammered.

"And your name?" the woman asked, trying to fill out the basic paperwork.

"What does that matter?" she asked in a frustrated, yet almost terrified, tone.

"Ma'm…" the woman started.

"Hey, Kelly," Aaron said coming up behind her.

"Oh, hey, Aaron!" the woman behind the counter said with a smile. The perky blond was thrilled to see Aaron Parker, especially since he'd been her high school crush for four years. Aaron knew that little tidbit, and he needed to use it right now for some leverage.

"Listen, can you do me a favor and get little Tyler here back to see the doc pretty quickly? We've got one shaken up momma here," he said with a sexy smile.

Kelly stared at him with a smile for a moment and then nodded as she buzzed them back into the triage area. After doing some minor clean up, the nurse put Tyler in a room as Aaron waited outside for him and his mom to finish up.

When she walked out of the room without him, Aaron looked concerned.

"Everything okay?"

"Yes. The doctor is just finishing up a couple of stitches. Poor baby just tuckered out, so he's asleep," she said with a tired smile. "Thanks for helping me back there."

Aaron waved his hand. "It was nothing. I heard him scream…"

"No, I mean at the front desk." She had a look of knowing on her face. She obviously knew that he knew something was amiss and she wasn't who she said she was.

"It's not my place to judge, Dawn. I mean, Dana? What do I call you anyway?" he asked with a laugh.

"Either one is fine," she said looking down. The doctor reappeared in the doorway.

"All finished up, ma'm. He's got a few dissolving stitches that will take care of themselves in a few days. Now, he's mighty tired, so I would check in on him several times during the night. I don't think he's got a head injury, but when they bang their noggin, it's always a good thing to check every hour or two. 'Course, if he starts throwing up or running a fever, you get him to the ER, okay?"

"Thank you, doctor," she said with a grateful smile as she reached her hand out to shake his. He held it for a moment longer and looked into her eyes.

"You're gonna be okay, ma'm," he said and walked off. She stood there stunned for a moment, shook her head and walked into the room to get Tyler. Aaron wasn't sure what the Doc meant, but it was like he knew that she needed to hear that she was going to be okay.

As they drove back to the campground, there were no words spoken between them. She was quiet, looking out the window as if she was looking into some other realm far away. They pulled into the driveway in front of his cabin and Aaron carefully unbuckled Tyler, carrying him toward the cabin instead of the camper.

"Where are you going?" she asked.

"Into my cabin," he said as he unlocked the door and pushed it open with his foot.

"Um, excuse me, but I want to take my child home.

He needs to rest," she said with her hands on her hips in the doorway.

Aaron placed him on the sofa and covered him with a nearby blanket as she stared at him dumbfounded. He motioned for her to come back outside so as not to wake Tyler.

"Listen, I don't know you very well. Actually, I don't know you at all. But that's not the point. The point is that Doc Clayton told you he has to be checked on every hour or two. You look completely exhausted already. There's no way you're going to be able to get up over and over for eight or more hours and check on him. What if you oversleep?"

"He's my child, Mr. Parker."

"Aaron."

"Fine. Aaron, he's my little boy. I can take care of him."

"I have no doubt about that. You're a terrific mother." Her eyes got wide and her mouth started to curve into the cutest little smile he'd ever seen.

"How do you know?" she asked trying to keep the smile from spreading across her face. It made him ache a little to think that she would question herself as a mother, of all things.

"Anyone can tell how much you love that boy. And how far you would go to protect him," Aaron said, realizing that he might be getting a little too personal.

"Yes, I would. Whatever it takes, I will protect him."

"Are you in danger?" he asked without thinking.

She turned toward the ocean and leaned her elbows against the railing of the porch as the ocean breeze blew her hair back against her shoulders. He heard a barely audible sigh and knew it wasn't the time to question her. Still wearing her swimsuit, Aaron realized she might be cold and uncomfortable.

"Listen, why don't you go grab some more comfortable clothing, and I'll put on a pot of nice, strong coffee?" he asked with a smile. She looked concerned for a moment, probably about leaving Tyler with a man she barely knew. "It's okay. I'll stand right here the whole time. You can watch me. I won't go inside with Tyler by myself."

She looked at him for a moment and then nodded her head. As she walked across the area between the cabin and her camper, she never looked back. Did that mean she trusted him already?

CHAPTER 3

Tessa closed the door to her camper behind her as she peered out the window to make sure Aaron was still standing on his porch. And he was. He was leaning against the railing looking out into the darkened ocean.

Man, he was sexy. She'd never met a man like him before. He just went into action as soon as he'd heard Tyler scream. It made her a little uneasy to think he might have been watching them on the beach. In fact, it made her a lot uneasy. It was exactly what she'd been afraid of. People were always watching, and that was what she'd been trying to avoid.

She gathered up some clothing and opted to take it back to the cabin so that she didn't have to leave Tyler alone for too long. It wasn't really that she was overly worried about Aaron hurting him. She just didn't want him out of her sight for any length of time. Aaron was right about one thing - she would protect her son with her own life.

She also packed some of Tyler's clothes since he was still in his damp swimsuit and headed back across the yard.

"Got everything you need?" Aaron asked with a crooked smile.

"I think so," she said.

"Well, if you forgot anything, it isn't like you're too far from home," he said laughing.

"Home," she said in a small voice. Was that what the camper was now? Home?

"You okay?" he asked in a way she wasn't accustomed to from a man. He sounded as if he really wanted to know if she was okay. Her heart felt warm for a moment at the thought of a man actually caring about her feelings. Realizing she looked like a deer caught in the headlights, she finally nodded quickly and then walked back into the cabin.

As they walked back inside, Tessa got a chance to look around. She wanted to know more about this Aaron person. He seemed nice and caring and strong, but then again so did her ex. *Every guy puts on a show at the beginning*, she thought.

The cabin was modest and rugged, but warm and inviting. There was a rock fireplace, hardwood floors and a deep, rich brown leather sofa. The handmade rocking chair in the corner seemed out of place at a beach. She felt almost as if she was in the mountains.

"This is a nice place," she said softly as she put her things on the chair.

"Thanks. It's not much, but I like to stay on site and

make sure things are okay around here. Care for a cup of coffee?"

"Sure."

"Cream and sugar?" he asked as he walked into the small kitchen and poured two cups.

"Both please. Who's this?" she asked pointing at a picture on the coffee table.

"That's my mom, Adele. She owns our real estate company, and this is one of her properties I took over a few years ago."

"I think I saw one of her signs on the way into town," Tessa said as she put the picture back on the table. "Are you an only child?"

"Oh, no. I'm from a big family," he said as he handed her the cup of coffee and sat down on the other end of the sofa. "I'm the youngest of five. Three brothers, one sister."

"Wow. That's amazing. It must be awesome to have so many people you can count on," she said without thinking. Trying to divert attention from her last statement, she took a sip of the coffee and put it on the table before standing up to check on Tyler. He was on the smaller sofa across the room, covered with a blanket and snoozing away.

"Are you an only child?" he asked. Now she wished she hadn't asked him a personal question first. This could only get more and more personal, and she needed to stay away from those kinds of questions at all costs.

"Yes. That's why I wish Tyler wasn't an only child. It can be a lonely existence," she said, again without the ability to stop her lips from moving. Why was she telling this virtual stranger so much about herself?

"I imagine so. In my house, it was never quiet. My Dad died when I was only two, so my Mom was constantly running around after all of us."

"I'm sorry about your Dad. I guess you don't remember him then, huh?"

"No, not really. I've seen pictures, obviously, but I don't have any of those cool father/son memories like throwing a baseball in the front yard."

For a moment, Tessa was immobilized. She could almost hear Tyler saying the same thing in twenty years. He would have no memories of his father if she had anything to do with it, but she'd be a terrible mother if she didn't at least realize that he would always feel a hole in his heart where his father should have been.

"You okay?" Aaron asked waving his hand in front of her face.

"What? Oh, yeah... I'm fine. Just tired I guess."

"Listen, why don't you get some sleep? I'll set my watch to check on him every hour..." Aaron offered.

"That's okay. I'm sure the coffee will kick in soon," she said with a forced smile.

"Boy, you really don't trust me, do you?"

"Don't take it personally."

"How could I?" he asked sarcastically.

Tessa felt terrible. Here was this sexy, nice man who had saved her son on the beach, yet she couldn't trust him. What had her ex done to her? He was still pulling the strings even when he wasn't around.

"Look, Aaron, this isn't anything against you. You have to trust me on that."

"I have to trust you?" he asked with a sly smile. "You could be some kind of sex starved ax murderer, and I've allowed you into my home."

"Are ax murderers typically starved for sex?" Tessa asked with a chuckle.

"Probably. I mean, why would they go around trying to kill people if they were having enough sex? I think they'd be more relaxed..." he said with a wink. Tessa suddenly found herself laughing. Actually laughing. Her sides started to hurt from the unusual muscle contractions. She hadn't laughed in so long, and she certainly hadn't experienced a belly laugh like Aaron caused.

Aaron looked at her intently as she wiped away the tears of laughter.

"What?" she finally asked as she took the last sip of her coffee.

"You're much prettier when you laugh," he said softly as he took her cup and went into the kitchen. Feeling like the air had been sucked from her lungs, Tessa said nothing.

~

AARON STEELED himself against the kitchen counter and took a breath. What was this woman doing to him? He felt good about making her laugh as it seemed she hadn't laughed in a very long time for some reason. But he hadn't remembered feeling so comfortable around someone in a long time either, and that was a strange feeling given that she was a total mystery to him.

He added more grounds to the coffee filter and put it back in place as he filled up the carafe with water. His plan was to stay up all night if she was staying up. He didn't want to leave her alone, but he also didn't want to be without her company.

"I've got more coffee brewing," he said as he poked his head through the opening between the tiny kitchen and the living room.

"Great. I think we'll need it." Her smile was still a bit forced, but behind it he could see that she really was a sweet, genuine person. She reminded him of a dog that had been kicked repeatedly by an owner and cowered away when anyone tried to touch him. For a moment, Aaron froze. Could she have been abused by someone? Not possible. Who would ever want to hurt such a beautiful, smart and sweet woman?

The coffee finished brewing, and Aaron refilled both of their cups before returning to the living room. He sat down and she looked up at him for a brief moment.

"What?" he asked.

"You're very nice," she said softly as she looked at the steam rising from her cup.

"Nah, just a regular guy," he said taking a sip.

"No, I've known lots of regular guys. You're…"

"Irregular?" he asked with a laugh.

"Well, yeah, I guess so."

"Hey!"

"I don't mean that as a negative thing. You're different. You're like a modern day superhero."

"Yep. I forgot to wear my cape today," he said putting his cup on the table.

"I'm being serious. You really helped me tonight. You have no idea how much." Her tone took a turn, and he could almost feel a sense of darkness hanging over her.

"I'm glad, Dawn... Dana? Jeez, I don't know what to call you..."

"Aaron, I..."

"It's okay, mystery lady. I don't need to know your name to know who you are."

"What?" she asked with a scared look on her face that made him sad and angry at the same time. Angry at whoever made her look that way.

"I know you're a kind and beautiful woman who loves her son more than life itself. I know you like coffee and the ocean. That's all I really need to know." She sighed as if she was relieved before Aaron added, "And I know someone has hurt you very badly."

Her face went pale, and her eyes welled with tears as she tried to turn her head away toward Tyler. He watched as her fingers grasped the coffee mug so tightly that the handle broke off and hit the hardwood floor with a thud. Tyler jumped from a dead sleep and sat up. "Mommy? Mommy?" he yelled looking around at the unfamiliar surroundings.

"It's okay, sweetie," she soothed as she jumped from the sofa, wiping the tears that had escaped. As she settled him and got him back to sleep, Aaron chided himself inside for saying anything. He'd made her cry which was the last thing he'd wanted to do.

A few minutes later, she'd gotten Tyler to sleep. Aaron was picking up shards of the coffee mug from the floor as she approached.

"I am so sorry," she whispered as she knelt beside him to pick up the little pieces. "I don't know how that happened..."

"It's okay, D..."

"Tessa."

"Tessa?" he asked with a smile as he looked over at her.

"Yes. My name is Tessa."

"That is a beautiful name. It fits you much better than Dawn or Dana," he said as he stood up and put out his hand to help her up. Much to his surprise, she took his hand and a bolt of electricity rocketed through his body. For a moment, they were close, face to face, as she looked up at him. There was almost a pleading in her eyes, as if she was asking to be saved from something that he couldn't see. Then she backed up a step and sat down.

"I'll replace your mug."

"No, you won't. It was an old mug anyway. I need some new ones, but I rarely have guests, so no one ever sees my crappy old dishes anyway," he said laughing.

"How did you know?"

"Know what?"

"That someone hurt me." She'd finally admitted it. Now there was no denying that someone had hurt this fragile, stunning woman named Tessa.

"Just a guess. You show some signs of abuse, Tessa." Her eyes started to well up again as she looked away. "Look, I'm not Dr. Phil or anything, but you can trust me. You can talk to me. I won't tell anyone, but it might do you some good to confide in someone. You've got to be lonely over there in that little camper."

"I am very lonely, but not because of the camper. I feel free in that camper, actually. Not safe, but free."

"I don't understand…"

"You've probably never been lonely a day in your life, Aaron. You have a great, big, happy family that loves you. Be thankful for that."

"I am very thankful for that, but it doesn't mean I haven't been lonely or betrayed before. In fact, it just happened to me."

"Oh?"

"Yes. Tell ya what. I'll share something with you that is very personal to me. I dated a woman for years, got engaged and then found her in bed with another man. Since then, I've been angry and lonely no matter who is around me. My family is worried about me, and my employees steer clear if they can."

"Really? You seem so calm and put together."

"Well, you've only seen the superhero side of me," he said with a wink.

"I like the superhero. Made me feel safe for a moment in time," she said standing up and looking at the pictures of his family lining the wall. "This is what I wanted for Tyler," she said pointing to a photo of Adele and all of her kids when they were younger.

"What?"

"I wanted a big family. I wanted vacations and front yard football games and picnics on the beach. But I didn't get that, and Tyler got a raw deal." Aaron was quiet while she talked. "It's funny how you have all these plans in life. You think you're going to conquer the world, become someone important…"

"You are someone important, Tessa," Aaron said standing up behind her.

"What?" she said turning around.

"You are the center of his universe." Aaron pointed at Tyler sleeping peacefully.

She paused and smiled. "I know, but I've let him down. You have no idea."

"It happens, Tessa."

"What does?"

"Life. Things happen. Kids are resilient. Whatever happened, it looks like you're trying to make it right. Make it better for Tyler."

"I am," she said as she sat back down on the sofa. "Wow, it's after one in the morning. This is going to be a long night."

"I'm wide awake. Why don't you lie down for awhile? You can sleep right here, and I'll keep watch."

"I don't know…"

Aaron stood up. "Here." He handed her his wallet and his keys.

"What's this for?" she asked laughing.

"You can sit on it or hide it or stick it down your shirt…"

"And why would I want to do that?"

"To prove to you that I won't leave. Those are my

only set of keys, that is my wallet and my mother's business card is in there. Adele Parker would kill me herself if she thought I'd kidnapped a child. I promise, he'll be fine. I'll set my phone to remind me to rouse him every hour on the dot."

Her face softened as she realized he was seriously trying to help her. She took the keys and wallet and slid them between her hip and the arm of the sofa.

"Why are you doing this, Aaron?"

"Doing what?"

"Being so nice and helpful to me? You don't even know me. You certainly don't have any responsibility for me or my son."

"Because I don't like bullies, and whoever has hurt you deserves to be beaten to a pulp. Tessa, no one is going to harm a hair on your head as long as I'm around, okay? So sleep. Rest. You need it." He stood up and retrieved a blanket from the hall closet and draped it across her body.

She looked like she wanted to say something, but instead opted to lie back against the sofa pillow. When she closed her eyes, she fell asleep within minutes. Aaron watched her, seemingly peaceful but probably filled with angst, and wondered how he had gotten himself involved in what could prove to be a dangerous situation. She was obviously running from something, or someone, and he had now put himself smack dab in the middle of it. But, for reasons beyond his comprehension, he wasn't scared. He was protective, almost fiercely protective, of a woman he'd just met.

～

TESSA WOKE up around six in the morning, unaware of how long she'd been asleep. The warmth of the blanket wrapped around her made her feel safe for the first time in years, as if she was in a cocoon of protection that couldn't be infiltrated.

She opened her eyes slowly as she saw just the smallest hint of light through the window blinds. The sun hadn't risen yet, so she sat up to see what she could in the muddled darkness. What she saw surprised her more than anything she'd ever seen before.

Aaron wasn't on the sofa with her. He was sitting on the floor beside Tyler, holding his hand while he lay sleeping against the arm of the sofa.

"Aaron?" she whispered as she crouched on the floor beside him. Groggy, he cleared his throat and opened his eyes.

"I'm awake. I'm awake."

"It's okay. Tyler looks good from what I can see. And he's snoring up quite a storm," she said smiling.

"I must have dozed off. I checked him at five thirty. What time is it?"

"Right at six."

"Good."

"Thank you so much for letting me get some rest. It's been... Well, let's just say it's been a very long time since I was able to rest." She smiled at him before standing up. "You have anything to make for breakfast here?"

"Sure. I've got some eggs and bacon. Let me..." he said as he started to stand up.

"No, let me cook it. It's the least I can do," she said as she made her way into the kitchen. Aaron followed her. "So, why were you holding Tyler's hand?" she asked as she took the eggs and bacon from the refrigerator.

"He woke up looking for you around three. He started to cry, so I held his little hand until he fell back to sleep."

Tessa stopped for a moment, smiled slightly and then broke the first egg over the frying pan.

"What?" he asked leaning against the counter.

"Nothing."

"No, what?" he pressed with a laugh.

"It's just that I'm not used to having someone around to take the pressure off during times like this."

"What about his father?" Aaron asked. Tessa stilled once again, but this time in fear. She knew that her body language was showing far too much about how anxious and terrified she really was, and she wished she could turn that off.

"Can we not talk about this?" she asked as she continued looking down.

"Okay. I'm sorry. It was just..."

"No, I'm sorry, Aaron. I know I'm not the easiest person to get to know." She turned and looked at him. "It's not you. I just have to do it this way."

He looked at her for a moment and then smiled. "Tell ya what. I won't ask any more personal questions, but you have to promise me that if you want to talk to someone, it will be to me. Deal?"

"Why does it have to be you?" she asked with a giggle.

"Because I know for a fact that you can trust me. The only way I can keep you safe from whatever is scaring you is to make sure I'm the only one you confide in." His words immediately made her feel better, but also vulnerable.

"Aaron, we're not your problem. We're just temporary tenants at your campground. I don't want you to have to be stressed out about my messed up life, okay?" She wiped her hands on the dish towel and pulled another frying pan from the cabinet next to the stove.

"Tessa, I'm a grown man. I like you and Tyler. You seem like nice people, and I don't take kindly to bullies. I don't know what you're running from, but I believe that you need an ally. Call it intuition. Isn't it okay for you to have a friend?" he asked. She nodded. "So, do we have a deal?" he asked holding out his hand.

She stared at his hand for a brief moment and then nodded again, shaking his hand. His handshake felt strong and confident, and she wished that she could feel that way. Something inside of her wanted to pull him toward her so she could rest her face against his chest and feel safe for just a few moments.

"So, tell me something. What's up with that camper you've got?" he asked as he pulled up a bar stool.

"What do you mean?"

"It's a little…"

"Beaten up?" she asked with a sly smile.

"Just a bit."

"It's all I could afford at the…" she started before realizing she might say too much.

"Gotcha. Does it have air?"

"No."

"Tessa! You guys have been living over there without air conditioning all this time?"

"Yes."

"It's too hot for that."

"We've been fine, Aaron," she said rolling her eyes as she flipped the eggs and checked on the bacon sizzling.

"I don't care. It's way too hot for you to be over there with Tyler. Y'all barely come out of that thing. How have you managed all this time?"

"When you've been through worse, the loss of air conditioning is not a big deal." Now she'd done it. She was saying too much again.

"What about your dog?"

"Oh crap! Beau! In all the ruckus last night, I forgot to let him out!" she said as she turned off the burners and started for the door.

"Relax. I'll go let him out. Does he need to be fed?"

"Yes. The food is in the cabinet under the sink. I can do it…"

"No, I don't mind. Besides, I would end up burning the eggs," he said with a wink as he quietly walked through the living room and out the front door.

CHAPTER 4

*A*aron made his way across the small yard
between his cabin and her camper. As he
walked inside, he was taken aback by just how old the
camper was. It looked like it'd been created sometime
in the 1970s with brown shag carpeting and harvest
yellow appliances. His stomach sank. What had this
beautiful woman and her son holed up in a tiny, old
camper for all these weeks? What in the world were
they running from?

Before he had a chance to think much more, the big
boxer dog came running from the back of the camper
barking at him. He jumped up on Aaron and almost
knocked him down.

"Hey, boy!" he said trying to calm the dog down.
Aaron had always loved dogs, but this particular one
seemed to be a little bit overzealous with his greetings.
He dug the dog food out from under the sink and
poured it in a bowl along with some fresh water. Then,
he clipped the leash that was lying on the kitchen table

onto Beau and walked him outside. Once Beau finished his business, he brought the dog back inside and allowed him to eat for a few minutes.

Aaron couldn't help himself. He looked around a little bit to try to get an idea about who this Tessa person was. Nothing in the camper said anything about her former life. However, just seeing what she was living in made him cringe. What had she left behind that was worse than this?

The camper was hot inside even though it was still early morning. There was no way he was going to leave the dog locked up in there all day without air conditioning, and he couldn't imagine how Tessa and Tyler had done it either. He grabbed the dog food bag and Beau's now empty bowls and started back across the yard, pulling the energetic canine at the same time.

As he walked into the cabin, Tessa was putting their plates on the breakfast table.

"Beau? Aaron, what are you doing?"

"It's already too hot over there, Tessa. I couldn't leave him inside that camper."

"But, Aaron…"

"Look, I don't have any cabins free right now. It's the busy season. So, you guys are moving in here with me."

"Um, no we're not. I have to draw the line…" she said.

"Look, I'm drawing a line. I own this campground, and I can't have dogs or people dying of heat exhaustion on my property."

"I don't want to be dependent on anyone. I don't want to be a burden."

"You're not a burden, Tessa. Trust me. I could use the company," he said smiling as he unclipped Beau and let the dog sniff around the place. Tyler started to rouse on the sofa.

"You want the company of a three year old and an unruly boxer?" she asked with her hands on her hips and a smile on her face. "That's your dream?"

"Yes, as a matter of fact it is. Just the other day, I was thinking to myself how I would love a toddler and a crazy pooch to help me really break this place in," he said putting his hands on his hips to mimic her.

"Very funny. I am sure something around here will get broken very soon!"

Aaron walked toward her and put his hands on both of her shoulders. "Don't worry," he said. She shuttered immediately at his touch. "Dang it, Tessa, what did he do to you?" he asked softly as he searched her eyes. He wanted to know where this guy was so he could beat him to a bloody pulp.

"Breakfast is getting cold," she said softly as she looked at her feet. "Tyler, you're up…" Tessa said when she heard a noise from the sofa. Tyler was sitting up getting a full face licking by Beau. Tessa walked over to him and sat down on the sofa, immediately inspecting his wound.

"Ouch!" Tyler yelped as Tessa touched the lump. "That hurts, Mommy! Where are we?"

Tessa looked up at Aaron who was standing in the kitchen doorway. "Well, we are right next door to our camper, but this nice man has allowed us to stay here overnight so you could get some good sleep after your boo boo." She rubbed his back with her hand as he pet Beau on top of his head.

"Mommy, when can we go back to the beach?" Tyler asked with his bottom lip poked out.

"Honey, I don't know…"

"Say, Tyler, do you like to build sand castles?" Aaron asked as he walked toward the sofa.

"I love to build sand castles!"

"Well, I am the reigning sand castle champion of January Cove. Do you think you could help me build a masterpiece out there on the beach today?"

Tessa stared at him, and he could tell she was battling within herself as to whether or not she wanted to allow Tyler back on the beach. He wasn't sure if it was for safety reasons or because she was scared of being found.

"Yes! Yes!" Tyler said jumping up and down. Beau was getting excited right along with him.

"Aaron, I don't know…" Tessa said as she stood up.

"Tessa, you're safe with me. I promise."

"You have no idea," she said softly.

"Hey, Tyler, why don't you go eat some breakfast. It's right there on that red plate," Aaron said pointing to the table as he and Tessa walked to the other side of the room.

"Listen, this is our life here, okay? You have no idea what could happen if I was found," she said. It was as much as she'd said during the time he'd known her so far.

"I'll keep you both safe."

"What are you? Some kind of FBI agent? Martial arts master? What makes you think you can keep us safe? You don't even know the situation, Aaron. Trust me when I tell you that we need to stay hidden from view. It has to be that way."

Aaron ran his hand over his chin, as he always did when he was deep in thought. "Okay, I have a plan."

"Why don't I like the sound of that?" she asked.

"My brother Kyle has a great place on the beach. His part of the beach is completely private, and we can have it all to ourselves."

"But won't he see us?"

"Yes, but he's trustworthy too. All the Parker men are," Aaron said with a wink.

"He won't know why I'm hiding."

"Neither do I."

"But you want to know, and so will he."

"No, he won't. I'll just tell him we want a quiet place to relax for the day. Tessa, no one needs to know if you don't want them to. Let's just go and allow Tyler to have some fun. One of these days, you're going to have to let go and relax. How will you ever live a normal life if you don't let your guard down at some point?"

"That's exactly what he wants, Aaron. When I let my guard down, I'm dead."

~

WHY HAD she said that of all things? Dead? Dear God, he wasn't ever going to let that one go. Time stood still as Aaron stood there looking at her, his mouth gaping open. She couldn't get a good breath into her lungs.

"Tessa, are you in that much danger?"

She wanted to say no. Say no, say no… "Yes." Damn it! Why had she said yes?

"You have to let me help you," he said softly as he watched Tyler feed Beau a piece of bacon in the kitchen. "For his sake, Tessa. Please."

"This isn't your problem, Aaron. I can't drag yet another person into it."

"Fine. Then I won't let either of you out of my sight ever again. Not until I know you're safe."

"Why do you even care, Aaron? You don't know me. You could walk away right now and never look back."

"No, I couldn't."

"Why?"

"Because I'm not that kind of man."

She wanted to hug him for just that one comment. But she couldn't involve him for the same reason she couldn't involve her own extended family. There was just too much danger.

"Please listen to me, Aaron. There is danger in this situation, and it's mine to deal with. I will protect my son just as I always have, but I won't involve other people. I can't. The guilt I feel for dragging my son through this is almost more than I can bear. Please don't make this worse."

He sighed and looked down. "Have you always been this stubborn?" he asked. Tessa laughed and threw her hands up.

"Some people would probably say so."

"So what is your long term plan then? To just keep running?"

"If I have to."

"What kind of life is that for you? For Tyler?"

"I can't think about that right now."

"You have to, Tessa. You're not thinking clearly. You're reacting out of fear instead of thinking logically. It's almost like you're running from a ghost instead of a person. How do you even know he's looking for you?"

"Trust me, I know. He doesn't like to lose or be made to look like a fool."

Aaron was growing frustrated; she could see it in his face.

"See? I'm already ruining your life, Aaron. Twenty four hours ago, you were single and footloose and fancy free..."

"Footloose and fancy free? What era were you born in again?" he asked laughing. She punched him lightly on the arm.

"You shouldn't have these worries. Your heart was just broken. You need time to heal."

"Being with you and Tyler has helped me already. It's given me something to focus on, to look forward to. That kid is a ball of energy, and I need that right now. I need a friend who understands and isn't a family member."

"You want me to be your friend?" she asked with her eyes wide.

"Well, it would be nice since I'd like to be your friend."

"I feel like we should be passing a note in class. Will you be my friend? Check yes or no," she said.

"So? Are you checking yes or no?"

"Okay, fine. But if we start to put you at risk or become a huge hassle in your life, promise you'll tell me."

"I promise," he said and then shook her hand. For a moment, they stood still staring at each other like each one knew a secret but didn't want to say it.

"So… I'm going to go give my brother a call and make sure that they aren't busy today, and then we'll pack up and head over to the beach. Sound good?"

"Yes, that's fine. But, I do need to go over and get some things from the camper, sunscreen and such."

"Okay. Just make sure that you keep your eyes open. Even though I don't know what you're scared of, I know that it requires you to be alert."

"Aaron, I appreciate everything you've done so far. Honestly, if I hadn't met you when I did…"

"Let's try not to even think about that, okay?" She nodded and then headed towards the door. Aaron sat down at the kitchen table and dialed Kyle's number. While he was sitting there, he watched Tyler continue to eat his breakfast like he was a grown man. That kid could certainly put away some food!

Kyle answered in his usually cheerful voice. He'd become a totally different person since he found Jenna again. They were madly in love and had created the perfect small family. Aaron expected them to announce their engagement any day now, and he knew that Kyle would want to have a big family with her. He was so jealous yet so happy for his brother.

"Hey man. How's it going?" Aaron asked.

"It's going great. To what do I owe this pleasure?" Kyle said with a chuckle.

"Listen, I was wondering if you guys mind if we used the private beach today?"

"We?"

"Yeah. I've got a new friend here at the campground, and I wanted to bring her and her son over for the day." Aaron knew that the wheels were already spinning in his brother's head even though he was trying his best to sound completely nonchalant about the whole thing.

"A new friend, huh?" Kyle said in a teasing tone.

"Don't start. She's just a friend. She's had a rough time lately, and her kid got hurt last night on the beach behind the campground. I don't want to take her back down to that area since it has some bad memories that are too fresh. Anyway, we didn't want to be out on a crowded beach with him running around because it's harder to pay attention to him." Aaron felt bad lying to his brother, but he was pretty impressed with himself for coming up with such a story on short notice.

"Sure, you know you can come over anytime. Jenna and I are going to be gone today. Mom is keeping her daughter so that we can get a little alone time, if you know what I mean." Aaron laughed at his brother's obvious joke.

"Thanks. We'll probably be by in about an hour, and we might stay until sometime after lunch."

"Sounds good. Enjoy." Kyle said. The brothers hung up the phone just as Tyler was finishing up his breakfast.

"What's your name?" Tyler asked cocking his head as he drank his orange juice and stared at Aaron.

"My name is Aaron Parker." Being the youngest, Aaron had never really been around kids much. He was always the baby of the family, and he wasn't totally sure how to interact with a three year old.

"Do I call you Aaron or do I call you Mr. Parker?" Tyler asked between slurps of his drink. He was pretty astute for three year old, especially one who had seemingly been through a lot.

"You can call me either one you want."

"My mommy says I need to call old men mister, so I guess I better do that."

Aaron stifled a laugh. "Yes. We wouldn't want to make mommy mad, would we?" He wondered how old Tyler thought he was. Maybe he needed to look into some wrinkle cream before he hit thirty years old.

"So this is your house?" Tyler asked.

"Yes. I own this whole campground where everybody parks their campers just like your mommy did. Everybody likes to come here and visit me at my campground."

Tyler stared at him for a moment and then hung his head. "We didn't want to come here, but we had to."

Aaron sat in stunned silence for just a moment. Was this boy trying to open up to him? He wasn't sure how much he should ask or say. After all, this wasn't his kid. It wasn't his place to intervene when it came to a child.

"You didn't want to come to my campground?"

"No. I wanted to stay at my house. All of my toys are there. But, my daddy did some mean things and we had to run away."

It tore Aaron's heart out to hear the little boy talk about something so huge and emotional. He was only three years old, yet he'd probably seen more in his little life than Aaron could imagine.

"You know what? You don't have to be scared anymore, Tyler. You see, I am a new friend of your Mommy's and I'm going to make sure that she's safe and you are too."

Tyler allowed a big grin to stretch on his face, and it made Aaron feel good that the little boy was more comfortable. At the same time, he hoped that he could keep his promise and make sure that they were safe. Before he could say anything else, Tessa returned with some extra clothing and was ready to go to the beach.

CHAPTER 5

*A*s they drove out to Kyle's beach house, they didn't get a lot of chances to talk. Tyler was excited and talkative all the way to Kyle's house. He pointed out everything along the way and asked what seemed like one million questions as any three year old would do.

Tessa seemed relaxed, which was a nice change of pace from the way that Aaron had seen her previously. She seemed to be settling in, but he knew that she was always on the lookout for whatever was chasing her. He wasn't sure if some person - likely her ex as Tyler alluded to - was actually going to come after her or if it was all in her mind, but he could tell she was truly scared. He wished that he could take that away from her somehow, but he knew he couldn't. Nothing he could say or do now would erase whatever had happened in her past.

A few minutes later, they pulled up at Kyle's house. Tyler bounded out the car like nothing ever happened to him and he didn't have a huge lump on his head. They carried all of their gear around the house and onto the private beach. As expected, no one else was there. The beautiful sand and blue waters always calmed Aaron, and he could tell that Tessa was taking it all in. She stopped for a moment and took in a deep breath. She'd worn a beach hat along with a long white flowing dress. She looked the perfect picture of a woman standing on the beach contemplating her life.

They started to walk closer to the water as Tyler ran toward it and started dipping his toes into the cold liquid.

"Be careful, Tyler! Don't go any further into the water until we get down there!" Tessa yelled. Tyler sat down and allowed the waves to roll over his tiny legs. Splashing around, he seemed to be oblivious to all the fear that his mother had.

"So what do you think?" Aaron asked as he sat their things down on the fluffy sand.

"This is beautiful. Your brother obviously has a very nice house. I love that big rock over there."

"Yeah. That rock actually has a lot of meaning to Kyle and his girlfriend, Jenna. They were high school sweethearts until they got separated for several years, and Jenna got married. It's a long story, but let's just say that they had many romantic interludes on that big rock. I would bet money on Kyle either proposing or marrying Jenna right on that spot." Aaron smiled.

"That sounds very romantic. I wouldn't know what that was like," Tessa said with a sad, far away look in her eyes.

"Why don't we focus on happier things? Let's make some new memories here on the beach for Tyler. I'm sure he's going to have some nightmares about what happened to him yesterday," Aaron said with a laugh.

"Probably not. He's a pretty resilient kid. Of course, I might have some very bad memories about yesterday," she said laughing. "He scared me to death. If you hadn't been there…"

"I thought we decided not to talk about anything stressful. Now, let's put some sunscreen on the kid and start having some fun!" Aaron said as he ran down toward the shore. Tessa followed him and lathered her son up with lots of sunscreen.

The next hour was spent frolicking and having a good time on the beach. Tessa seemed like a different person, laughing and giggling like she was a young child herself. Aaron was so happy to see that, but he was especially happy to see her let go of the fear for a little while. She knew she was safe with him on that private beach, and he hoped that he could give her that feeling of safety more often.

What was he thinking? He'd only just met this woman hours ago, but he was protecting her like she meant something to him. The realization hit his brain quickly – maybe she did mean something to him. Aside from her stunning good looks and great personality, he felt an enormous attraction to her that he didn't expect. This wasn't just about being a Southern gentleman or chivalrous. Instead, this was about protecting someone he'd grown to care about in just the last few hours. How was that even possible?

He thought it was crazy at first, but then he realized he'd been with Natalie for years and didn't know her any better when they broke up than he did in the beginning. That much was obvious when he realized that she cared little for him and could cheat so easily. Why couldn't he fall in love with somebody so quickly? Wait a minute, love? What was he thinking?

"Are you about ready to get some lunch?" Tessa asked around noon.

"Oh, sure. We could go grab something at the diner." Tessa's face went white, and for the first time that afternoon he saw the fear return.

"Aaron, I can't. It's too risky," she whispered.

"You can't go to a small-town diner? Are you sure?"

"Positive. I know he's looking for me, and I can't take any unnecessary chances. You've done so much for us already. Just take me back to the camper and I'll make something for Tyler and me…"

"You have got to be kidding me. You guys are not going to go eat lunch in that tiny, hot camper."

"I don't understand you. Why are you doing all of this for me? I mean, come on, you just met me hours ago. It's not like I'm your girlfriend or your wife or your sister. I'm not even a close friend. You have no reason to go out of your way to protect me." Her tone wasn't one of anger or irritation. It was more like she was completely confused by his actions.

"How about I just say that my mom raised me to be a good man. Isn't that enough?"

"Your mom must've raised you to be a great man. You're not the typical guy, trust me."

"Don't worry, you'll see my flaws soon enough. I told you, I want to be your friend. I'd like to be able to redeem the male species for you." He winked at her which almost drew a smile from her face, but not quite.

"Well, I'm not sure you'll ever be able to do that but I'm willing to give it a try. I just don't want you to threaten your business or your life hanging around with the likes of me." She hung her head, much like Tyler did at the kitchen table, and it made Aaron cringe inside.

"Hey," he said putting his finger under her chin and making her look at him. She jumped just a little bit, but he was careful to be gentle and not too forward with her. "I may have only known you for a few hours, but I'm a good judge of character. You're a good person, Tessa, and I'm not in the habit of allowing good people to be bullied by anyone. You don't have to be my wife, girlfriend or sister for me to want to protect you. Someone should've protected you a long time ago."

He wasn't sure, but he thought he saw tears welling up in her eyes. She turned her head quickly to look at Tyler who was still splashing around in the waves. The last thing he wanted to do was make her cry. Crying women always confused and unnerved him.

"How about that lunch now?" she asked again. "Maybe if I keep my beach hat on, I won't be seen as easily."

"This might be a stupid question, but wouldn't the man that you're talking about recognize your son? I mean, if we're out in public and Tyler is with us, won't he know who you are?"

Tessa looked stunned for a moment and then shook her head. "See? I'm not even thinking logically anymore. We can't go out with Tyler or it'll be very obvious that it's me. I feel so trapped." She put her hands over her face and growled.

"What you can't do is stay in the house all the time. We've got to do something. It seems to me that waiting for this mystery man to make his move is the wrong way to go. What we need to do is figure out a way to protect you for the long-term without you having to look over your shoulder all the time. We either need to do it legally or illegally, but I prefer legally."

Tessa's mouth dropped open. "What are you saying? You want us to do something illegal?"

"No. That wouldn't be my first choice, but you can't go through the rest of your life being scared all the time, Tessa. I know you don't want to tell me what happened, but you've got to tell somebody eventually. You've got to take care of this long term. You can't keep you and Tyler and a dog cooped up in that old, crappy camper with no air conditioning. Don't take this the wrong way, but part of your job as his mother is to make sure that he has the best future possible, right?"

"Of course."

"Then we have to take some proactive measures to make sure that happens. That kid has probably already had plenty of fear instilled in him in his first three years of life. I hate to see you going around being scared and pushing that anxiety off on him. He needs a stable, normal life." As soon as he'd said it, Aaron regretted it. Making her feel guilty hadn't been his intent at all.

"Don't you think I know that?" Tessa was obviously getting angry. "When I ran off from my ex, the first thing I considered was giving my son up for adoption. Isn't that crazy? I love him more than life itself. I would protect him, and I did protect him, with my own life. I was so willing to give him up to someone else just so he would have the opportunity at a normal life. I even drove to an adoption facility and made an appointment with someone. When I went to meet with the person, I chickened out right there in the parking lot. I sat there in that ratty camper with my son playing with his blocks in the back and decided I couldn't go through with it. Maybe that was selfish of me."

"No, Tessa. That wasn't selfish. You're his mother. He should be with you. You've got to let me help. You already know you can trust me, right?" He leaned down and looked into her eyes.

She looked at him for a moment as if she was considering the question and then allowed a small smile to escape her face. "Of course I do. I didn't know if I did at first, but I'm absolutely sure I can trust you now."

"Then you have to tell me. It might seem like I'm some kind of small-town Joe, but trust me when I tell you that I have connections that can help us figure out what to do next. I'm not talking about the mafia or anything crazy like that, but I do know people who can help us deal with this legally the right way. But I can't deal with the unknown. I need to know the full story."

"It's so hard to relive it, Aaron. I don't know if I can do it."

"You said it yourself. You'll do anything for Tyler, and you have to do this for him."

She nodded, looked at Tyler playing on the beach and then looked back at him. "Okay, I'll tell you the whole story. But first, we've got to get somewhere alone. I don't want him to have to remember all of that."

"Okay. If you trust me, then would you trust my mother?"

"What do you mean?"

"My mother raised five kids by herself, and she would love to have Tyler over for a few hours while you and I go somewhere to talk." Tessa took a deep breath as if this was another scary moment in her life and finally nodded her head.

"If you trust her, and I know you do, then I trust her."

~

TESSA COULDN'T BELIEVE that she had agreed to allow Aaron's mother to watch Tyler for a few hours. Never in her wildest dreams a few days ago would she have believed that she'd go along with something like that. But, for whatever reason, she had grown to trust Aaron immensely in the short time that she'd known him.

She figured that anyone who raised a man like him must be a great person. In all reality, she was kind of interested in meeting this Adele Parker and finding out more about her. She hoped that she could be a mother as good as Mrs. Parker was.

Lately, though, she wasn't so sure. She knew that she made the right decision getting herself and Tyler out of the situation with her ex, but she wasn't sure what she was going to do from now on. She really hadn't thought the plan out in advance, just jumping and running as soon as she had the chance. Sure, she'd saved her money, but she hadn't been sure exactly when she'd be able to leave.

And now she had to tell Aaron the whole story. It was going to be one of the most difficult things she'd done because she would have to relive it all over again. She knew that she couldn't ever get it out of her mind or forget what happened, but she was hoping to be able to move forward without ever having to speak of it.

After finishing lunch that they picked up in a drive through , Aaron headed toward his mother's house. He called her from the beach to make sure that it was okay to bring Tyler by, and Tessa hoped that Tyler would go along with the plan. He was usually pretty good at welcoming new people. He never really had grandparents, so he hadn't been around older people. Of course, Tessa wasn't sure how old Adele was, but she was certainly older than anyone Tyler had probably ever met before.

The fact that their lives had been so sheltered didn't help when it came to teaching Tyler about the world. He was almost like a blank canvas having never really been out and around a lot of other children and people. The thought of it made her sad inside because she didn't grow up that way. She had friends and relatives and lots of fun times, but Tyler hadn't experienced any of that. His life had been closed off from the moment he was born and Tessa was determined to make sure that the rest of his life was an open book full of friends and family and love and new experiences. But Aaron was right. She couldn't give him that kind of life if she was always on the run.

"Everything okay over there?" Aaron asked as they drove down Main Street toward his mother's house. She'd been awfully quiet since they left the beach, full of thought and full of angst. She wanted to tell him everything, but she wanted to say nothing. It was an internal fight that she was having with herself that could never be solved. One side of her was going to get hurt today no matter what. He'd taken her to a small, out of the way sandwich shop and gotten take out so that they could eat it in the car. She felt like a first class loser.

"Yeah. I'm just tired and full. Lunch was great." She knew that he wasn't going to believe that everything was okay, but he also knew that Tyler was in the back-seat listening to every word they said. For a three year old, he was very smart and able to pick up on all kinds of emotional nuances.

"We're almost there. My mom lives just down here on the corner. She's very well-known in town, and I know she's going to love you and Tyler. She loves little kids, and it's been awhile since she's had some around. Of course, she wants grandchildren as soon as possible, but my brother Kyle has given her one already by getting back together with Jenna."

"I'm sure she does love children if she raised five kids alone."

"Well, she didn't do that on purpose. When my father died, she was left to take care of everything by herself. She started in real estate under another company and supported us all those years on one hundred percent commission. When she started her company, she finally got some financial stability but we were older by then."

"Well, I admire her already for a couple of reasons."

"You do?"

"Yes. For one thing, she took care of the five of you on her own. For another, she raised a good man in you." Aaron smiled and winked at her before returning his eyes to the road.

～

As THEY CAME around the last corner, Tessa could see Adele's house. She started to get nervous in the pit of her stomach, but she knew this was something she had to do. It was amazing the turn that her life had taken just in the last few days. Meeting Aaron had been a wonderful thing for her and Tyler, but the thought of opening up to him was starting to sound like it might be too much. At the same time, she knew that she had to or else Tyler's life would be forever ruined. He'd be stuck in the same shell he was stuck in when she lived with her ex.

"Here we are."

"Wow! This is a big house!" Tyler exclaimed.

"Well, it kind of had to be because I have three brothers and one sister."

"I wish I had a brother or sister. It gets lonely being the only kid in our family."

"You never know, you might have a brother or sister one day. Until then, you have to keep your mommy entertained all by yourself." Aaron winked at Tyler and pulled the car into the driveway.

Tessa sat still, saying nothing and staring straight ahead.

"Ready?"

"I think so." She turned and looked at him, and as if sensing her anxiety, he reached over and squeezed her hand once before opening his door and stepping out. He walked around and opened her door, a chivalrous, Southern gentleman move that she had never experienced before first hand. She'd seen it in movies and heard about it, but no man had ever walked around and opened up her door before today. She slowly stood up and stared at him closely, face-to-face.

For a moment, she could feel butterflies in her stomach and heat rising through her core, but she assumed that it must just be extra adrenaline or left-over anxiety about meeting his mother. That's what she wanted to tell herself, but her heart and mind said differently.

"Thanks."

"For what?" he said in a whisper.

"For opening my door."

"You shouldn't ever have to say thank you when a man opens your door. Any man who's with you should open your door for you, Tessa. A real man is willing to do anything for a woman he cares about." She half-heartedly smiled and nodded her head as he closed her door and pointed towards the front steps.

They walked up the stairs and into the house, Aaron calling his mom's name. She came down the stairs with a big bright smile on her face. Adele Parker was beautiful with blond hair and a petite frame. Tessa hoped that she would look that good when she was her age, although she didn't feel that way right now. She felt like she was one hundred years old after all the stress that had come along with her life in the last few years.

"Well, hey there! You must be Dawn, and you must be Tyler. My name is Mrs. Parker." She was full of energy, and Tessa couldn't believe that she had recently been in the hospital. Aaron had told her all about that on the drive over, although she didn't have much to say since she was lost in her own thoughts most of the time.

"Hi. So nice to meet you," Tessa said shooting a glance at Aaron. He had told her that her name was Dawn, and she wondered why he did that.

"Welcome to my home. Tyler, I hear that we're going to spend some time together this afternoon. Let me ask you something. Do you know how to bake chocolate chip cookies?" she asked him kneeling down and smiling.

Tyler grinned from ear to ear and started jumping

up and down while clapping his hands. "I sure do!" he said.

"Well good 'cause I'm going to need some extra hands in the kitchen. I've already got my friend, Kaitlyn, in there up to her elbows in cookie dough," she said smiling at Tessa. "I love to bake dozens and dozens of chocolate chip cookies and take them around to the local fire stations. Do you think you might want to help me do that today?"

"Yes, ma'am!" he said as he grabbed her hand and followed her into the kitchen. Aaron stood there grinning and threw his hands up in the air.

"Did you see how she just completely ignored me? She loves little kids more than anything, but it was like I wasn't even standing here!" Aaron said laughing.

"Tyler just took right to her. That makes me feel so much better. But why did you tell her my name is Dawn?"

"I figured it was the best thing to do just in case your ex come sniffing around. My mom won't know who Tessa is, so she won't be of any assistance to him. I'm just trying to protect you and her at the same time. I hope that's okay."

"It's more than okay, Aaron. I'm so thankful that you thought about that because I didn't. I really need someone with a level head helping me with this because I'm not thinking clearly about everything I need to do to make sure that Tyler is safe."

"Yes, you need for Tyler to be safe but you also need to be safe yourself. And that's what I'm here for. That's what friends are for, right?"

Tessa nodded her head, but she wasn't sure why she felt a little sad inside when he said the word friend. Was that all they could ever be? What was she thinking? She just gotten out of a tumultuous, violent relationship and here she was starting to develop feelings of attraction to her new friend. She needed a friend more than she needed a boyfriend, so she was determined to push those feelings aside and think of Aaron as nothing more than someone who was helping her.

"So where are we going today?" Tessa asked.

"I have a place in mind where we won't be interrupted and we won't have to worry about anybody finding us. Do you trust me?"

"Of course I do, but why can't we just go back to your cabin?"

"Because I run that place, and my guests and employees won't leave us alone if they see my car there for long. If we're going to go somewhere and talk and really think out the logical steps to getting the situation resolved, we need to make sure that we're uninterrupted and no one will find us. I have the perfect place."

"Okay, if you say so."

"Let's go tell Tyler goodbye and get on the road."

CHAPTER 6

*A*s they drove down the road toward Aaron's mystery destination, Tessa couldn't believe that she'd left her son in the care of someone she'd only just met. It shocked her as much as it probably shocked Aaron, but she was desperate. It scared her a little bit because any other time that she'd been desperate in her life, she'd made some very poor decisions. She hoped that she was making the right decision now by telling Aaron everything and allowing Tyler to stay with Adele. She sighed lightly, thinking of how she was so sick of second guessing every decision in her life. Why couldn't she just be a normal twenty-something woman with normal twenty-something problems?

The one good thing she had going for her was that Adele Parker was very known in January Cove. Her signs were everywhere, and she raised five children on her own. She had to be a pretty good woman to create children who were doing so well in their lives.

"So, no clues as to where we're going?" she asked with a sly smile.

"You even know this area?" Aaron responded with a laugh.

"Nope. Not a bit. I sort of ended up here by default. We rolled into town on fumes, and I saw a sign for your campground before it was too late. In fact, I'm not sure how I'll ever move the camper off your land."

"Well, I can always push it up to the road," Aaron joked. "Of course, I'm not even sure a homeless raccoon would want to live there."

"Gee, thanks," she said, lightly punching him in the arm.

"So, tell me a little something about yourself, Tessa. First of all, what's your last name?"

"Why does that matter?" Her guard immediately went back up like a fortress around a castle.

"Because if I'm going to help you, I'm probably going to need your name. Tessa isn't exactly enough information to go on," he said.

"My last name is Reeves.

"Good to know. Tessa Reeves. I like that. It's nice."

"I'm glad it meets with your approval," she said smiling. "So you tell me something about yourself then."

"What do you want to know?"

"Tell me about the relationship that went sour."

"I've already told you everything there is to know.

"I don't think so. You gave me the Cliff Notes version, but there has to be more to it than that. Were you really in love with her?"

"I thought I was. When all was said and done, I

think I was more in love with the idea of being in love with her. I'd really like to settle down and have a family, and I thought we had that kind of relationship. I'm glad that I know now that she wasn't the kind of woman I want to spend the rest of my life with, but it didn't make it any easier to go through all of that."

"Does she ever try to contact you?"

"You know that's two questions. I get to ask you another one," he said with a wicked smile.

"Fine. Ask away. I can't promise that I'll answer, but you can ask," she said with her own sly smile.

"You have family?"

"You mean like a mom and a dad?"

"Yeah."

"My mother passed away when I was ten years old, so I was raised by my father. Unfortunately, my father got into some trouble when I was a teenager and ended up in prison. He died there when I was nineteen years old. That's when I met my ex, at my lowest point in life."

"I don't hear from her anymore."

"Who?" she asked.

"I assumed that you wanted the answer to your previous question. Her name is Natalie, and I don't hear from her anymore. I see her around town with different guys, but I don't care to hear from her."

"You shouldn't want to talk to someone like that. Anyone who could hurt you must not be a very good person," she said offhandedly.

Aaron looked at her with a grateful smile and then returned his eyes to the road. "Thanks."

"It must've been hard to grow up without your father."

"Yeah, but I never really got a chance to know him. I was only two years old when he died, so I only know him through the stories that my mother tells and pictures. I assume it was a lot harder for you because you got to spend the first ten years of your life with your mother."

"It's never easy to lose a parent, but it was especially hard to lose my mother. I was an only child and I felt like I lost my way after that. A girl needs her mother, and my father just went downhill after she died. It was like he lost his will to live and started doing all kinds of stupid things that messed up both of our lives."

"So that's how you ended up with your ex?"

"Partially, I guess. I didn't have a good sense of direction when I was a teenager or in my early twenties. I didn't have a mother to teach me what to look for in a man, and I didn't have a good father to show me the kind of man that I should be looking for. I guess I was just lost, and I didn't have a lot of self-esteem. I suppose I don't have a lot of self-esteem right now either, but at least I realize it."

"Here we are," Aaron said as he pulled onto a long gravel driveway.

"What is this place?" she asked as they went around the big curve and faced a large, white antebellum house.

"This is a place that my mother owns. It's actually an investment property that used to be a bed-and-breakfast. Right now it's empty, with the real estate market being what it is. I thought we could come here and spend some time talking without being interrupted. There are few people who even know this place is back here these days," he said.

"It's beautiful. I've never seen an antebellum house up close like this. It's very majestic," she said.

"I've always dreamed of living here, but that would require me to move away from the campground which I really can't do right now."

"Why can't you move away?"

"Well, first of all I have no one there that I trust to run it by themselves. And secondly, I don't feel like I need a house this big unless I'm going to have a family of my own. Now I seem to be further away from that goal than I ever was, so I really don't need all this space."

"Maybe things will change. I hope they do, Aaron, because you deserve all good things."

"Thank you," he said as he reached over and squeezed her leg lightly. The touch of his hand sent shock waves up and down her body. She'd never felt such a spark from a man's touch before, and it almost made her shake.

"Shall we go in?" she asked trying to break the tension in the car that was building. How was she so attracted to this man that she'd only just met, and how could she ever be sure that her ability to choose a man was correct?

Aaron unlocked the front door and waved Tessa inside. The home was beautiful and ornate, and a bit sad from being empty. The winding staircase in the foyer reminded her of Gone With The Wind, and she could imagine the regal parties that were hosted in this house during the Civil War era.

"Let's go into the parlor. We still have some furniture in there," he said pointing to a room on the right.

"The parlor?" she said with a chuckle.

"Hey, that's what my mother calls it. I don't feel very manly saying it, but…" he said with a shrug. Tessa sat down on the red velvet sofa and Aaron sat down next to her, putting his leg up onto the couch so he could face her.

"Okay, I guess this is as easy as it's ever going to be for me to give you this information. My biggest concern is that you're going to think less of me, and I wouldn't blame you if you did. My story only shows what a weak woman I am."

"That can't be, Tessa. I've already learned so much about who you are, and your past doesn't matter to me. As far as I'm concerned, you have a clean slate with me."

"Thank you for saying that, but I'm not sure you'll feel that way once you hear the story," she said as she took in a deep breath, steeling herself for a moment. "I met Ethan when I was nineteen years old just after my father died in prison. He was ten years older than me at the time, so I guess I looked up to him. Ethan was a new officer on the police force in our town, and he had run ins with my dad on multiple occasions. My dad hated him, and I hated my dad at that time. I felt like he'd screwed our lives up and he made my name mud in our small town by all of his antics.

Right after my father passed away, I was living in this little efficiency apartment that I could afford while waitressing at the local diner. That's when Ethan came by one day to express his condolences, or at least that's what he was pretending to do. It wasn't long after that when he asked me out on our first date and we started being known as a couple around town.

Things moved really quickly for us, but the abuse didn't start immediately. Looking back now, I can see he was grooming me for what was to come. He always had a problem with anger, but it wasn't directed at me until much later. After we had dated for two years, he proposed to me. By that time, I knew he wasn't who I wanted to spend my life with, but I was afraid to tell him. His anger was getting worse and worse, and he had this power trip thing going on.

I finally agreed to his proposal, but we never set a wedding date. Instead, I found out that I was pregnant and things went downhill quickly. The abuse actually started while I was pregnant with Tyler. He didn't care that I was pregnant, but he didn't really want us to have a baby. He pushed me down the stairs a couple of times in an effort to try to make me miscarry, but thankfully it didn't work."

Aaron's face crinkled up as he listened to her story. He didn't interrupt, but instead allowed her to keep talking no matter how hard it was for him not to reach over and comfort her or scream or yell about the idiot that she'd been with for all those years.

"When I was pregnant with Tyler, he started holding me captive. He told everyone that I left him and left town. But that wasn't true. I was actually locked in our basement. He'd set it up so that I couldn't get out, couldn't have access to the outside world and I didn't even have medical care for Tyler. He wanted me at his beck and call, and that included fulfilling any of his sexual needs at any time. He was very rough and violent with me, and because I didn't have any extended family left that I was in contact with, no one was ever looking for me."

Aaron couldn't hold back anymore. "Dear God, Tessa, I'm so sorry. Why on Earth would he have become so angry with you?"

"Around that time, an old friend from middle school, a guy, found me on Facebook. We were chatting about old times, nothing major. In fact, my friend is admittedly gay. Ethan still got jealous. He said I wasn't going to make a fool out of him. He was very impressed with what he perceived as his 'place' in the community, and he was sure that I had slept with this old friend of mine and gotten myself knocked up. I offered a DNA test, but he said no way, he didn't want his name dragged through the small town mud. So, instead, he concocted this plan to punish me and keep me locked away from being 'social' with other men."

"This is just so unbelievable to me…" Aaron stammered. She kept talking for fear of chickening out.

"As I got closer to delivering Tyler, it became apparent that he was going to have to allow me to have the baby. But again, he didn't want any of his police buddies or anyone else knowing that I was still around and he certainly didn't want anyone to know that I was having a baby. So, I gave birth in a bathtub in our basement and had to take care of Tyler by myself. I had a very difficult delivery, but he didn't even come downstairs. I felt like I was in some kind of a third world country where a woman is forced to give birth on her own. Thankfully, my body cooperated with me and I didn't bleed to death, but I never did get any medical care that I needed for Tyler."

Unable to contain himself, Aaron spoke. "I can't believe what you're telling me. Why would this man want to hurt you so badly? Why wouldn't he love his child? Surely he knew it was his if you offered a DNA test..."

"Aaron, you're thinking like a normal man. He's not a normal man. In fact, I believe he's sociopathic. He seemed to take great joy in keeping us captive there, and watching me go from an outgoing woman to a shell of my former self. It was awful, but I tried to get away so many times when I was pregnant. Once Tyler was born, my options were limited as I couldn't get both of us out of there easily without being noticed. He had us locked down like prisoners of war."

Aaron asked why her coworkers weren't looking for her.

"You've got to understand, I was from a small town just like January Cove. You see, everyone there really respects law-enforcement, as they should. No one had any idea that he was so sick and demented. Plus, there's a lot of incestuous relationships in the police force there. Everyone is family. In fact, his father and brother are both police officers, so I knew they'd never believe what he was doing. They all really thought that we'd broken up and I'd moved on. I had no options because I knew if I got out of there and tried to run, he'd just find me and kill me. He said so many times. He had no problems killing me and Tyler."

"So that's why you ran. You didn't feel like you had any options to go to the police. God, Tessa, you must've felt so alone and terrified when you saw daylight after three years…"

"It was… and is… terrifying. If I'd gone to the police there, it would've only resulted in me getting killed. He would never let his name be smeared like that."

"So how did you finally escape?"

"I overheard him on the telephone saying that his father was in the hospital. His dad had a heart attack, and I knew he would go to be by his bedside because they were very close. So, I knew that was my only opportunity to try to get out. He had everything locked down and nailed shut. I had to work very hard over the course of several hours to pry open the door leading upstairs. I was terrified."

"I'm sure you were," Aaron said as he slid closer and put his hand over hers. Suddenly, she felt a wave of safety come over her that she'd never felt in her life. He might as well have thrown his body over hers to shield her because that's exactly what it felt like.

"Once I finally pried the door open, I gathered together what little belongings we had. He would occasionally buy us clothing from a thrift store that was two counties over, but we never got anything new which is why I'm always wearing these old, unfashionable clothes," she said as she pulled at her skirt. "I had also been putting away a little bit of money here and there that I stole out of his wallet when he was asleep. Of course, I'd have to have sex with him in order to get him to go to sleep anywhere near me." She cringed as she said the words.

"He never noticed you were stealing money?"

"No. But, you have to keep in mind that I was stealing very little at a time. A dollar here or five dollars there, but nothing big. I didn't want to tip him off. It took me months to get enough money to take with us, and I was able to find that nasty old camper for a very cheap price. I literally bought it as we were walking out of town."

"How far did you have to go on foot?"

"We walked about three miles before I saw the camper parked in someone's front yard with a for sale sign on it. Believe it or not, he sold it to me for two hundred bucks just to get it off his lot. I put a little money in gas, and it brought us all the way here to January Cove. We stopped here because this is as far as I could go on the gas money I had. Then, I bought a little bit of food at your store and paid the lot rent in advance for three weeks at your campground. I don't have any money left, so I don't know what we're going to do next."

"You know I'm going to help you, right?" Aaron said looking into her eyes as he took her hand between both of his. He was strong and masculine and steady, and she desperately needed that right now.

"You don't have to. As I said before, this isn't your

problem. You wanted to know what happened, and I'm telling you. I think you deserve that much after all that you've helped us already."

"And as I said before, I'm doing this for you and Tyler. He's never had a normal life, and that boy has a light inside of him that deserves to shine. I intend to do everything I can to make sure that happens."

"So what do we do?" she asked sighing as she leaned back on the sofa. His hands slipped away from hers, and her heart sank when she no longer felt his touch. What was that about, she wondered to herself.

"The first thing I'm going to do is call my sister," Aaron said standing up as he reached into his front pocket in search of his phone.

"Your sister?"

"Yeah. She actually used to date a private investigator. I think the first thing we need to do is get a track on this guy to make sure that he's not heading toward this area. Do you think he'd hire anyone else to do his dirty work?"

"I certainly wouldn't put it past him. After all, he has access to criminals anytime he wants, but I think he'd rather do the job himself. He's probably extremely angry at me right now and feeling like I got one over on him. He won't just allow that to happen. He's going to come after me. There's no question about that."

"Then we need to get on this fast. Here, I brought this notebook. Write down his full name and as much personal information as you have. I'll call Addison and we'll get to work on this."

Tessa looked up and smiled. "Thank you. No one

has ever tried to help me. I don't know what I did to deserve finding you as a friend, but I will thank God every day for it."

"Well, get used to it. That's what friends are for, right?" Aaron whispered as he handed her a pen.

"I think this is going a little beyond the typical friendship," she said without thinking.

Aaron fidgeted for a moment. "What do you mean?"

"I just mean that I've never had a friend who is willing to help me protect myself from a deranged ex," she said with a laugh trying desperately to change the subject.

"Oh." Was that a hint of disappointment in his voice?

"Do you have any idea why he wanted to hold you captive rather than just letting you get on with your life?"

"He was highly jealous. He didn't want anyone else to have me if he couldn't. I wanted to leave, to get out of the situation I was in, but he wasn't about to let that happen. He would date women and actually bring them home, have sex with them and then come force himself on me. It was a power trip."

"But why wouldn't he have wanted Tyler?"

"I don't know, he was angry with me I guess. He also didn't want anyone to know that he was holding me captive, so he would've had a hard time explaining this new baby boy. As time went on, I noticed he was drinking more and I'm pretty sure he was taking drugs too, so he was just out of control all the way around."

"Tessa, I'm so sorry that you had to deal with this. I

promise I'll do whatever I can to help you. You're not alone anymore."

"Aaron, I don't want you to put yourself in harms way because of me. It's bad enough that Tyler and I are always in danger, but you and your family don't deserve this. I'm telling you that he's crazy and will do anything to get back at me. You can still walk away from this. You can still forget you ever met me. Because there is a chance you could get hurt trying to protect us."

"I'm willing to take the chance," Aaron said looking in her eyes as he reached out and touched her hand again. "Don't you know you're worth fighting for, Tessa?"

She stared at him and then looked down without answering. The emotions building up in her chest were overwhelming her ability to speak or think. "For now, I'm going to go make a call to Addison and give her this information. Hopefully, her friend will be able to help us out and find out where he is right now. As long as we can keep track of him, you'll at least have some semblance of peace."

"I suppose, but there's always the chance that he's got one of his goons after me. It might not be him, but I really think he would want to do this himself."

"Hey, maybe we'll get lucky and he won't seek vengeance," Aaron said with a shrug.

"We won't get that lucky."

≈

As Tessa sat in the living room, she could hear Aaron on the phone in the kitchen. He was talking to his sister who was giving him information on how to get in touch with her friend. A few moments later, she could hear him making that all important call to the friend whose name was Stan from what she could understand.

After a five-minute conversation, Aaron came back into the living room with a smile on his face.

"What? Is there news already?" she asked.

" No, it just feels good to have something underway."

"Yeah, it actually does. What did you tell him?"

"I didn't go into specifics. The less that people know, the better. I just told him I needed to keep track of someone, so he's looking into it right now. While we wait to hear back from Stan, I had a plan for us to do something," he said smiling and rubbing his hands together.

"A plan?"

"Yes. There is a part of this property that I'd like to show you."

"Okay…"

"Don't worry. We'll be safe way out here. No one knows this place is back here, and we can see them coming before they ever get to us."

"I'm not worried, Aaron. I feel safer right now than I have in years." She looked up into his gorgeous face and he reached out to pull her up from the sofa.

"And don't worry about Tyler. I just texted my mom

and she said he's doing fine." He squeezed her shoulder as if to comfort her.

"I'm not worried about Tyler either. You have to understand, I haven't had a family in a long time, and I never really had a normal one. It feels good to have people helping me for once. I know it won't last long, but I really do appreciate it right now."

"Why do you say it won't last long?"

"Because you're not my real family. I don't expect you to take on my problems and help me out in the long term."

"Tessa, you've got to stop this."

"Stop what?"

"Putting this wall up around you. It's okay if people care about you and help you. Let me care, okay?" he said softly as he rested his hands on her shoulders. Every nerve ending in her body lit up at his touch, but she wasn't about to show it. Still, her heartbeat sped up and she was sure she might hyperventilate at any moment.

"But how can you care about me? You don't even know me. I understand that you're just being nice like you would to anyone."

"That's not true. I don't help everyone like this. In fact, I didn't want to be around anyone after my breakup. When you met me, I was coming home from a self-imposed exile to the mountains. I was trying to calm myself down, get rid of the anger. I was trying to be alone, so I certainly wasn't up for helping anyone."

"Then why me?" she finally asked softly, wondering

if it was the wrong question to pose to someone who was trying his best to protect her.

"I don't want to scare you."

"Scare me?"

"Yeah. Because it might make me sound like a lunatic or a stalker myself," he said with a little laugh.

"Come on. Tell me."

"Well, when I saw you out in the rain wrestling with your dog, I couldn't help but notice how beautiful you are. After having gone through such a heartbreak recently, it was nice to see a beautiful woman and watch her smile. Then, when I saw you in your swim-suit down by the shore with your son, I can't say that I wasn't a little bit attracted to you."

She started to smile and looked down at her feet.

"So you're helping me because you think I'm pretty?"

"No. It helps, but no," he said with a smile. "I'm helping you because I like you, for one thing. I think you're a nice person, and I really like Tyler. And like I said before, I hate bullies. So, I'd like for you to stop questioning the reasons why I'm helping you if you don't mind."

"Okay. Fair enough. I'll stop asking. So where do you want to go then?"

"Come on, I'll show you. I don't want to ruin the surprise." She smiled, and for the first time in a long time she was excited to be surprised about something. All of the surprises that she'd had in most recent years were not good ones. Like the surprise of finding out that her ex was an abuser or the surprise that she was going to spend years locked in the basement of his home, unable to see anyone.

They went out to the car and he opened the door for her. "We have to drive there?"

"This is a huge property, so walking would take too long and we'd be tired before we even got there."

"Okay," she said as she slid into her seat and watched him walk around the vehicle.

They drove down the long gravel driveway deep into the woods behind the house. A few moments later, she could see an opening and what appeared to be a body of blue water.

"What's that?" she asked with all of the enthusiasm of a small child seeing the ocean for the first time.

"That is a blue spring. At least that's what we call it. Some underground springs come directly from the ocean and feed into this small pond."

He walked around and opened the door for her before she could get out. She wasn't sure if she'd ever get used to the chivalrousness of a true Southern gentleman, but she was sure willing to try.

"This place is beautiful," she said as she looked around and tried to take in all of the scenery. With the lushness of the green trees and the beauty of the sparkling blue water, she'd never seen anything like it.

"We used to come down here and fish when I was a kid sometimes. The cool thing is that some of the aquatic life from the ocean filters to the springs over here so sometimes I'll see things like little crabs running here along the shore," he said pointing to the ground.

"It's like your own private oasis," she said. She thought to herself how nice it would be to have a private spot where no one could find her, but she also knew that it would be short-lived. She wasn't about to put Aaron or his family in harm's way, so she couldn't tell him that she planned to get the heck out of Dodge before her ex found her.

CHAPTER 7

*A*aron wasn't used to having a woman to care for like Tessa. Natalie had never really needed him, but it felt good to be needed. As the youngest of his siblings, he'd always longed to have a brother or sister to care for, but he was the baby. It was kind of nice to be able to comfort Tessa and tell her everything was going to be okay.

It'd only been a couple of days since he'd known her, but he felt a fierce sense of protection that went far beyond just being a Southern gentleman. Of course, his mother had instilled in him that he was supposed to be chivalrous and protective of women in general, but this was something else entirely.

He also wasn't accustomed to feeling such strong feelings for someone in such a short period of time. Even with Natalie, it had taken years to get to the point to where he wanted to propose marriage. A part of him would always believe that he only did it because he was getting older and felt like it was time to settle down.

He thought to himself how strange it was that those feelings of anger that he had toward Natalie had dissipated in the last two days as his focus had shifted. She no longer seemed relevant to him, and he felt ambivalent about her even taking up space in his mind anymore. Maybe it was just a good distraction to have Tessa and Tyler around, but he couldn't convince himself of that.

"So what are we going to do?" she asked with a smile on her face.

"See that canoe over there?" She looked across the shoreline and then back at him.

"Seriously?"

"Why not?"

"I've seen a lot of people tip over in those things! What if we fall in?" she asked with a giggle.

"Then we'll dry off." He laughed and then realized that she really was a little bit scared of going out on the water with him in a canoe. Maybe he shouldn't push her, he thought, but he really wanted her to have an afternoon to enjoy herself before his sister called back with whatever news she would have about Tessa's ex. "If you don't want to…"

"No, it's okay. I want to," she said nodding her head as if she was trying to convince herself.

"Don't worry. I go out in canoes all the time. I'm an old pro," he said as he walked backward down the shore to get the canoe. Not looking where he was going, he tripped on a rock by the shore and hit the ground like a sack of potatoes.

"Aaron!" she yelled as she ran toward him, but she

also tripped and fell right on top of him, both of them just inches from the water nipping at the land.

"Are you okay?" Aaron asked, pulling her long hair away from her face as she struggled to hold up her head. "Tessa?" he said softly. She was laughing so hard that she couldn't speak and then buried her head in his chest. He joined in her laughter and put his arms around her.

"I'm so sorry..." she said between breaths. "I thought you were hurt, and then I tripped..."

"It's okay. This has been the best thing to happen to me in months," he said with a chuckle, and that only sent her into further hysterics. "You have the best laugh I've ever heard," he said softly as she turned her face up to his. Never in his life had he wanted to kiss someone so bad. He could almost taste her full lips, and he wondered what those lips could do to him in other places. As if she sensed his inappropriate thoughts, and maybe the inappropriate things his body was starting to do to him, she slid backward and up onto her knees next to him.

"Um, maybe I should help you get the canoe this time," she said with a nervous giggle.

"Tessa," he said as he touched her arm and sat up. "It's okay. I'm not expecting anything from you, okay?"

"I wasn't... I didn't..." she stammered.

"You're beautiful and funny and sweet and smart, and I'm a man. But you don't have to be nervous around me. I don't take what isn't mine like that jackass of an ex did. You belong to you, Tessa. Don't you ever let any man take that control from you again, you hear me?" he said with more intensity than he meant to project. Her eyes welled up, and there he was again - about to make a woman cry.

"You're like a Hallmark card. How do you know the right thing to say every single time?" she said softly as she blinked her eyes quickly to stop the tears.

"I don't. Trust me. Several women might disagree with you on that one," he said with a wink as he pulled both of them to their feet.

"Well, apparently some women are too dumb to know what they have," she said quietly as she walked toward the canoe. Aaron's heart quickened for a moment, but he pushed the comment to the back of his mind and helped her slide the canoe into the water.

～

SHE WAS BEAUTIFUL. No doubt about it. And he was going to get screwed again. Somehow, some way, she would break his heart just like Natalie did, but it wouldn't be her fault. It would be some jackass abuser named Ethan's fault, and he'd like to put his fist into his...

"You okay over there?" she asked, breaking his thought - which was probably a very good thing.

"Just enjoying the scenery," he said, looking directly at her.

"Yeah, it's stunning out here. The trees, the blue water..." She seemed oblivious to the fact that he was talking about her. She thought so little of herself, and it pained Aaron. How did some idiot get so much power over her for so long? "You love the outdoors, don't you?"

"Yes. I'm definitely the outdoorsy one in our family. I was always outside as a kid, finding bugs and building tree houses. Broke my arm twice in the same year falling out of trees."

"Seriously? Ouch! I've never broken a bone. Not adventurous enough, I guess," she shrugged.

"Breaking bones is for idiots, and I was definitely an idiot as a kid. I have three older brothers, and they loved to dare me to do stuff. One time, Kyle dared me to climb onto the roof to get a Frisbee he'd thrown up there. My Mom came outside just in time to see me fall into the bushes. I was all scratched up, but I only broke a toe that time. Miracle."

"That is a miracle! It must have been nice to grow up with siblings. Someone always has your back," she said as she watched the oar he was rowing with glide back and forth in the water.

The trees shaded the pond just enough that only slivers of sunlight were coming through, and the breeze was just enough to blow the soft waves of her hair across her bronzed shoulders. Afraid she would catch him staring at her, he finally spoke. "Siblings are great, except you have to share everything with them. Like Christmas. When we were struggling for money, Christmas could be very slim pickings, and my mother would have to spread the gifts out between five kids. She was far too proud to ask for help from anyone. Sometimes, I'd get jealous of friends at school who had both parents and got lots of gifts..." Suddenly, he felt like a jerk. Here he was complaining about not getting enough Christmas presents as a kid when Tessa had lost both parents and been abused. "Damn, Tessa, I'm so sorry. I should have thought before I spoke," he said, putting the oar down and running his fingers through his hair.

"Why?"

"Because I didn't have it anywhere near as bad as you did. What am I complaining about?"

"Aaron, we all have things that make us upset or sad from our pasts. We all have stories. No one person's story is any less legitimate than another's. I wasn't thinking anything bad about what you were saying at all. I was just enjoying your stories." She smiled the most genuine smile at him, and it made his heart ache for her. How could any man have had a woman like this and spent every waking hour trying to make her *not* smile? *Not* feel loved. It was beyond his comprehension.

"Do you have any good memories from your childhood?"

"Oh, of course I do. Before my mother died, we had a great family. I was their only child. My mother was told she could never have kids, so I was a miracle."

"You still are," he said softly without thinking. "Oh, crap, did I say that out loud?"

She giggled. "Yes, you did. And thank you. That is the nicest thing anyone has ever said to me in my life."

"Really?"

"Really. You're such a sweet guy, Aaron. How could that nasty woman have done what she did to you?"

"Not everyone thinks I'm sweet, Tessa," he said as he picked up the oar again. "I've got my faults. I'm stubborn and opinionated at times."

"I see that as strong minded and self directed."

"How do you do that?"

"Do what?"

"Still see the good in things after all that has happened to you?"

"Because I have to, Aaron, or I'd go crazy. There is good in the world and in people. You just have to find it."

He stared at her for a moment, wishing he knew what to say. There was no way he could take her painful memories away or make things better. He could only wait for Stan to call back with an update. He felt helpless, yet he knew he was all that was standing between her and total despair.

～

IT WAS all getting too close and personal, but she couldn't help but feel comfortable around Aaron. He seemed kind and sweet and generous, but then again she'd thought Ethan was a decent person. She never thought of him being particularly kind or sweet or generous for that matter, but he seemed okay. He seemed safe. Oh, how wrong she'd been about that.

Aaron had been quiet for a few minutes, rowing against the calm of the blue springs. She'd never seen a place so beautiful in her life. It was the most peaceful place on Earth, she was sure of it. She felt very secure here, like no one could ever find her. Yet she knew that Ethan could find her anywhere on the planet if he wanted to.

"Whatcha thinkin' about?" Aaron finally asked.

"About how this must be the most peaceful place on Earth," she said, recounting her thoughts.

"It definitely ranks at the top. Sometimes I come here when I need to think."

"Did a lot of that recently, huh?"

"Oh, yes. If these trees could talk," he said with a wink. "The thing is, you can come out here and yell at the top of your lungs and no one is going to hear you. Why don't you try it?"

"Yelling?" she asked, putting her hand on her chest in shock.

"Sure. Sometimes yelling helps get all the emotional crap out. Don't you have some pent up anger you'd like to unleash?"

"Of course, but I'm not doing it here... in front of you." She shook her head and laughed nervously.

"Okay, but what would you yell if you could? I mean, what would you say to your ex?"

"I'm not sure I could put words to the anger I feel toward him. And myself."

"Tessa, you have to know that getting abused wasn't your fault. Right?" She looked at him a moment and nodded her head ever so slightly.

"Logically, I know that. If another woman told me this story, I would tell her it wasn't her fault. But when it comes to myself..."

"You're too hard on yourself. You did the best you could in a bad situation."

"Maybe, but I worry what people will think of me. They'll wonder why I was so weak that I couldn't break out of that house. They'll wonder what I did to deserve it."

"No, they won't, Tessa. He's a cop. He has a gun. You had a baby to protect. People will understand that and support you."

"What about your mother, Aaron? The woman lost her husband and raised five kids on her own. Don't you think that she would look at someone like me and wonder why they didn't have enough backbone to get out of that situation?"

"Absolutely not. My mother would applaud you for making it through what you did, Tessa. She'd call you a wonderful mother and a strong woman who waited until the time was right and made a bold move to take her life back. She'd call you a survivor, Tessa."

"Maybe, but look where my life is, Aaron. I'm hiding out in a nasty camper with my little boy and a very rambunctious dog. I'm relying on help from strangers. I have no money, no gas to get anywhere, no extra food. Yeah, I'm quite the catch."

"Tessa…" he started to say, but he was interrupted by the ringing of his phone. Their eyes locked for a moment as if both of them knew that there was no turning back. Chances were good that either Addison or Stan were on the other end of that phone. "Hello?" Aaron said as he carefully pulled his phone from his pocket.

Tessa sat and listened to one end of the conversation. She could hear a man's voice on the other end, but she couldn't hear what he was saying.

"Okay. Well, listen, it's really important that you keep your eyes on him. If he moves, you call me immediately. Day or night, okay? No, we're not involving the police yet. And don't tell my mother or anyone else. The less everyone knows, the better. Thanks, man." Aaron hung up the phone and put it back in his pocket.

"Well?" she asked anxiously.

"It's good news, for now at least. He seems to be at home, and it doesn't look like he's packing up to leave or anything. Stan said he saw him about a half hour ago, and he's got a guy doing surveillance right now."

"But, Aaron, how long can that go on? I can't afford to pay someone to watch Ethan for the rest of my life." She chewed on her bottom lip, an old anxious habit, and sighed.

"I'm paying Stan, Tessa."

"Aaron, you're too good to be true, and I am so thankful that you're here to help me. But even you have to admit that watching Ethan long term isn't the answer."

"True. So what is the answer?"

"I don't know. I really don't know. I feel like I'm still in prison. He's still got me because he's in my head. As long as he is free and breathing air, he's still got me captive," she said, unable to stop the tears from rolling down her cheeks. "It's not fair."

"Nothing about what happened to you is fair," he said as he leaned in and took both of her hands. "But we're going to make this right somehow. I promise." She looked into his eyes and believed him, but she wasn't sure why. It seemed like Aaron could make everything right, but then again she didn't want to trust a man like that again. It hadn't served her well in the past.

"Aaron! The oar!" she yelped as she watched his knee bump it into the water.

"Crap!" he yelled as his automatic reaction made him lean to try to catch it. Instead, the canoe started to wobble back and forth violently while he tried to stabilize himself. Again, they locked eyes for a brief second as each of them realized that they were going down whether they liked it or not.

The canoe tipped on its side, throwing both of them into the water. Aaron was on the outside, but somehow Tessa got stuck with her head under the boat.

"Tessa!" he yelled as he swam a couple of feet to her and pushed the boat back upright. She was gasping for air, panic stricken from falling and then getting sucked under the toppled canoe. He slid his arms around her waist and held her close to his chest as she caught her breath. Wearing her white dress, she felt like she was in a wet t-shirt contest on a crowded Spring Break beach.

"I'm okay," she whispered, trying not to look at him for fear that he would see the attraction in her eyes. Just holding her upright and pulling her close was enough to make Tessa want to hug him back or kiss him or worse. He had a quiet confidence and strength that made her feel more secure than she ever had.

"You sure? Can you swim?"

"Yes. Unless I'm having a panic attack at the time!" she said with a giggle, finally mustering the courage to look at him. They were nose to nose, and she could feel his warm breath floating across her cheek as he spoke.

"I'm so sorry. I'm normally very good with canoes. I think you make me nervous," he said, his voice soft but husky. For the first time, she noticed his dimples and wanted to lick one. Mentally slapping herself across the face for thinking that, she tried to divert her attention to something else. Maybe those full lips of his?

"You're starting to make me nervous too," she finally managed to say. "Guess we'd better start swimming for shore?"

"Can you grab onto the canoe?"

"Yeah," she said reaching her right arm out and pulling it closer.

"We can't climb in from out here. It'll just topple over again. But there's a rock over here that we can climb onto and then get back into the canoe. You just hang onto the canoe, and I will swim us to the rock."

Slowly but surely, Aaron pulled himself, Tessa and the canoe all the way to the rock. She was amazed at how strong he was and it sent electricity rocketing through her body to think of what else he could do.

When they reached the rock, he picked her up around her waist and hoisted her onto the rock. As he tied off the canoe, she checked her dress and had her worst fears confirmed. Not much was hidden under the gauzy white garment.

Aaron climbed up on the rock beside her, and she noticed him noticing her.

"My dress... Not a good day to wear white..." she said as she fumbled with the straps to keep them pulled up under the weight of the water saturating her clothing.

"I'm not complaining," he said softly as he looked at her eyes. He was out of breath, still panting for air from the swim. He pulled his navy blue t-shirt over his head, twisted it to get as much of the water out as possible and handed it to Tessa. "Here. Cover up." She smiled, and then slid the shirt over her head. For the first time, she got a real look at his taut muscles. He was blond, but tanned from working outside so much. His abs were solid and she could see an actual six pack for the first time in her life. Ethan didn't have a six pack, and the thought of seeing him without clothes made her shudder. "Why, Miss Reeves, are you checking me out?" he asked with a dimpled smile that made her want to touch those muscles and more.

"What? No, of course not. I thought I saw a mosquito on your chest," she said. *A mosquito on his chest? Really, Tessa? Way to think on your feet. Duh.*

"A mosquito, huh?"

"Yes. That's my story and I'm sticking to it," she said, realizing that she'd been caught. "What about you? You certainly noticed my dress clinging to me for dear life."

"Guilty as charged. I'd have to be dead not to notice a gorgeous woman with a wet, white, clinging dress on." They both started laughing at the predicament they were in. "I'm supposed to be protecting you, and so far today I've made you fall and almost got you

RACHEL HANNA

drowned." He ran his fingers through his hair and sighed.

"And I still feel safer with you than I've ever felt," she responded softly.

"You do?" he asked, kicking his foot across the water.

"I do. This is the most peaceful I've been in years, Aaron. From the time I was ten, my life has been tumultuous to say the least. The past couple of days has given me a little hope that I might have a normal life at some point."

"You will, Tessa. You deserve a great life, and so does Tyler. It will happen, but it might take some time. We just have to come up with a plan. Let me ask you something. Do you have any proof that he was holding you captive?"

"Proof?"

"I mean, I believe you one hundred percent, but the police are going to want to see proof. How can they be sure you weren't off somewhere else for three years and had a baby?"

She pondered his question for a moment. The truth was, she didn't have much of anything. Obviously, they could find her DNA in the basement, but it would have been there anyway since she lived with Ethan. She hadn't been allowed to have a phone or a computer, so she had no photos or videos to prove anything.

"That's the problem. I have nothing, and he knows it. He knows he can do whatever the hell he wants, and I can't prove a thing."

"That's not true, Tessa. We'll figure something out."

"How can you be so sure?"

"Because I have to be," he said bumping her shoulder. "But, for now, I think we should take some time to think. To plan."

"How much time?"

"A week. All of this is so raw and fresh for you, and maybe you will think of something that we can use on him if you just have some time to think. You need space to feel safe and secure for a bit so you can relax."

She thought for a moment about what he was saying, and he was exactly right. It was like he was reading her mind. She'd been so consumed with escaping and keeping Tyler safe that she hadn't been able to calm herself down until this moment.

"You're probably right. I need some time to focus on what to do. Maybe I'll think of something. But we can't keep taking up space in your cabin, Aaron. It's not fair to you, and I'm sure it will raise some eyebrows with your employees."

"I don't care what anyone thinks, Tessa."

"I know you don't, but I do. I cannot have it on my conscience that I gave you a bad reputation," she said, bumping his shoulder in return.

"Trying to protect my virtue, are you?"

"Absolutely."

"I don't think we have to worry about that, but if it makes you feel better, why don't we move over here for a week? It'll be like a little mini vacation for me. I love this place."

"Seriously?"

"Yeah. It'll be nice to spend some time teaching Tyler how to fish in this spring. Has he ever fished?"

She looked at him, and then it registered in his face that Tyler had never really learned anything outside of that basement.

"Oh, God, Tessa... I'm sorry. I wasn't thinking straight."

"It's okay, Aaron. Tyler hasn't had a chance to learn much of anything."

"Well, that's my new goal. For the next week, we're going to let that kid have a blast. I'm gonna teach him to fish and make paper airplanes and make the best ice cream sundaes..." Aaron was rattling off all of the cool things he was going to teach her son, and her heart literally skipped a beat. She was practically filling up with pride at the kind of man Aaron was even though she had nothing to do with it.

Tessa kicked her feet back and forth in the water like a kid. "This has been really nice."

"Really? I haven't scared you off yet?"

"It takes a lot more to scare me off, Aaron," she said rolling her eyes.

"So, are you in agreement to staying here for a week?"

"Can I bring Beau?"

"Of course."

"Would you say no to me about anything, Aaron Parker?" she asked batting her eyelashes.

"I doubt it, Tessa Reeves."

CHAPTER 8

*A*fter spending awhile sitting on the rock chatting, Aaron realized it was getting late and they needed to pick Tyler up from his mother's house.

"I guess we'd better get brave and try to get back into the canoe," he said nodding toward the old boat.

"You sure?"

"Not really. I'm not very confident in my skills at the moment."

"Lovely," she said laughing. Without warning, Tessa put her foot into the canoe and jumped across, narrowly escaping turning it over again.

"What are you doing, crazy woman?" Aaron said.

"I took charge. I'm gonna save us both," she said proudly with her hands on her hips. She was perched with her feet on each side of the floor of the canoe, holding her hand out to Aaron.

"My hero," he said with a wink as he took her hand and pulled the canoe closer. He got one foot in, but the canoe started to tip, and he didn't want to chance dumping her out of it all over again.

Aaron slid into the water and started to pull the canoe across the spring. "Why didn't you get in?" she asked.

"Because I don't want to dump you out."

"But now you're all wet again."

"I'll dry off, don't worry."

He looked up at her as he paddled, watching her now dry hair float in the breeze. It had a natural curl to it, but not enough to look kinky or frizzy. No, it was perfect just like everything about her. And that was the real danger in all of this. He wasn't worried about his physical safety, but about the safety of his heart. She was a shattered woman, and he hoped she wouldn't shatter him at some point.

When they finally reached the shore, she climbed out, gingerly avoiding the rocks that dotted the shoreline of the small spring. Aaron crawled to the shore and then stood up. She removed his blue shirt and handed it to him, and if he didn't know better, he would've thought she was trying not to look at his chest. It made him want to smile, but he forced his face to stay still.

"You don't need this anymore?"

"No. I think my dress has dried enough," she said softly as she looked down to check. He could no longer see through it, so it was at least dry enough to make her feel comfortable.

"Damn it!" Aaron said as he reached into his pocket and dug out his drenched, non-working cell phone.

"What's wrong?"

"My phone. It's toast."

"Which means Stan can't reach you if Ethan moves…"

"Right. We'd better load up and go pick up Tyler before it gets too late. I'll call Addison from Mom's house and get Stan's number again."

"Sorry about your phone," she said with a sly smile.

"Then why are you about to laugh?" he asked as he poked her in the arm.

"Because you make me laugh, Aaron Parker."

~

THE RIDE back to Adele's house was quiet, and Tessa's mind was racing. How was she already starting to feel things for Aaron? She barely knew him, yet here she was making a potentially stupid mistake by getting too close too soon. Was she just starting to rely on him because she had no one else? Was he really as great as he appeared to be?

Tessa had had a lot of time to think during those three years locked in her basement. She thought about how stupid she was for trusting Ethan, and how she'd never make that mistake again. She'd never let a man "rescue" her and make her depend on him like Ethan had. She wouldn't fall for charm or wit or kindness. She vowed to become hardened and tough and independent. The only problem was, she had no idea how to do that.

"Everything okay?" Aaron asked as they drove into town.

"Huh? Oh. Yeah. I'm fine," she stammered, worried that he was reading her thoughts.

"You're awfully quiet."

"Just thinking. I do a lot of that," she said looking at him and smiling.

"I bet. Three years is a lot of time to think." How did he do that?

"It is. I've had plenty of time to beat myself up over the last few years."

"Can I say something?"

"Sure."

"I'd be willing to bet that you think you don't make good decisions. I'd also be willing to bet that you're worried that I'm some jackass in disguise like your ex."

"Well, I…"

"And that would be totally understandable," he said. "But, here's the thing. You're gonna have to trust someone at some point. If you let that jerk taint who you are inside, he's already won. He will have you imprisoned forever. Trusting is more courageous than walling yourself off forever, Tessa."

She knew he was right, but she wasn't sure she could do it. Trust again? Dangerous, she thought.

A few minutes later, they pulled into Adele's driveway. Aaron walked around and opened her door, as usual. Before they could get into the front entryway, Tyler came bounding toward them with a grin on his face and chocolate on his cheeks.

"Mommy!" he squealed as he hugged her waist tightly. She leaned down and picked him up.

"Hey, sweetie! I'm guessing from the chocolate on your face, you had fun?"

"Yes! We made cookies and took them to the fire department! Kaitlyn helped me too."

Adele came from around the corner with her apron on and a smile on her face. "He did great!" she said ruffling his hair as she walked into the foyer. "What a sweet boy he was. The firemen even let him climb inside their truck. He said he'd never seen a fire truck before. I was surprised," she said with a hint of concern in her voice.

"We lived in a small town," Tessa said quickly before shooting a glance at Aaron.

"Listen, Mom, can I borrow your phone? I dropped mine in the water."

"Aaron, you've always been a klutz, son," she said shaking her head. "Sure, you know where it is."

As Aaron walked into the kitchen, Tessa stood there, unsure of what to do.

"Dawn, would you like to sit down for a few minutes?" Adele asked. Tessa didn't turn around at first. "Dawn?"

Realizing her mistake at not recognizing her fake name, she turned around.

"Who's Dawn?" Tyler asked with his head cocked to the side.

"Your Mommy's name is Dawn," Adele said with a laugh as she sat down in a chair in the front room.

"No it's not, silly!" Tyler said as he scooted out of Tessa's arms and ran back into the kitchen where Kaitlyn was mixing more cookie dough.

Tessa froze in place, a look of fear overtaking her face. Adele stared at her for a moment before patting the chair next to hers. "Come. Sit," she said sweetly.

"Aren't baby boys wonderful?" Adele said.

"Of course. Tyler is a hand full, but the biggest blessing in my life," Tessa said as she sat down.

"Well, Aaron is my baby boy, you know?"

"Yes. I'm sure that love never changes, Mrs. Parker."

"And neither does the protectiveness a mother feels for her children, Dawn." She raised an eyebrow when she said her name, and Tessa knew her cover was quickly being blown.

"Tessa. My name is Tessa."

"Why did you lie, Tessa?" she asked softly.

"Because I'm in hiding. I'm protecting myself and my son, Mrs. Parker."

"Please, call me Adele."

"Okay, Adele," she said with a slight smile as she looked down at her hands.

"Someone hurt you?"

"Yes. For a long time. And he's going to try to find me. I ran away."

"Good for you, Tessa," she said, surprising Tessa completely. "And my son?"

"He found out and has been trying to help me. I told him not to, because it could be dangerous..."

"I probably don't want to know more. I had a mild stroke recently," Adele said with her hand on her chest.

"Oh, God, I'm so sorry. I shouldn't have said anything. I didn't mean to stress you out," Tessa said sitting at the edge of her chair.

"It's okay, honey, I'm not that fragile. But no mother wants to think of her baby in danger. I'm sure you understand." Adele smiled.

"You're right. I'm sorry I brought him into this, Adele. I'll make it right, I promise," Tessa said as Aaron walked back into the room. Adele opened her mouth to say something, but Aaron cut her off.

"Ready to go?" he asked.

"Everything okay?" Tessa asked.

"Yep. Except I need to go get a new cell phone," he said laughing. "Maybe we can stop by the cell phone place on the way out of town. See you soon, Mom," he said, kissing her on the cheek. Adele looked at Aaron with such love, and it broke Tessa's heart. She'd just dragged this wonderful woman and her family into the middle of her mess, and she had to do something to stop it.

～

"YOU'RE BEING QUIET AGAIN," Aaron said as they neared the campground. Tessa had barely said a word all the way home, while Tyler jabbered on about everything he'd done all day.

"Just listening to my son," she said softly.

Aaron didn't buy it, but he wasn't going to press her in front of Tyler. After stopping by the phone store and activating his new phone, they arrived back at the campground to pack up some things for their stay at the other house.

Tessa went to the camper immediately and packed

up what little they had while Aaron took care of Tyler and the dog. An hour later, they were on their way back to the other house. Still, she was quiet.

"I think we should get some groceries so we can minimize our trips into the city," Aaron said, stopping at a small grocery store just before they left town.

"Sure. Good idea," she said, glancing two doors down at the pawn shop. "Listen, would you mind taking Tyler with you? I wanted to look for something at the pawn shop."

"The pawn shop?" Aaron asked with a questioning look on his face.

"Yeah. I'm looking for a lighted makeup mirror. Unless you have one?" she said with a smile.

"Um, no. Just be careful, okay?" he said softly as he took Tyler's hand and went into the store.

"I will," she said, and then she walked toward the pawn shop. Aaron wondered what she was really up to as she didn't wear much makeup, but he had to get Tyler into the store.

About fifteen minutes later, Tessa joined them in the grocery store like everything was fine. He decided not to press her on it. Maybe she was just feeling comfortable enough to venture out on her own for a few minutes since Ethan was being watched.

"Anything in particular you want?" he asked her as they walked up and down the aisles. Tyler was bouncing around, eating a lollipop that Aaron had bought him at the front of the store.

"I'd love some marshmallows," she said with a grin.

"Marshmallows?"

"Yes. They used to be my favorite guilty pleasure, but I haven't had them in... years," she said with a sad smile.

"Then marshmallows you shall have, my lady," he said with a wink as he grabbed three bags from the shelf.

"Three bags? I'll be a whale!" she said trying to put back two of the bags.

"Listen, I want to make sure that Tessa Reeves never has to live without marshmallows again, okay?" he said holding them above her head. "Now, really, you're making a scene!" Tessa started laughing, and he realized it was the most genuine laugh he'd ever heard in his life.

"Y'all are gonna get in trouble!" Tyler said between licks of his lollipop.

"Oh, yeah?" Aaron said picking him up and putting his nose against his. "Let me ask you something, mister. Have you ever heard of s'mores?"

"Some mores? Nope."

"Close enough. Well, they are just about the yummiest thing on the planet. But, you have to make them over a campfire or else they aren't the good kind. They have marshmallows and graham crackers and chocolate..."

"Yum!" he said wiggling in Aaron's arms.

"Yep. Super yum. How about we make some tonight when we get to the other house?"

"Okay!" he squealed as Aaron put him down.

"Operation Show Tyler Everything is officially underway," he whispered into Tessa's ear with a grin.

"You're gonna spoil him in the next week, aren't you, Aaron Parker?"

"I'm going to try my best," he said bumping her shoulder as they continued down the aisle.

~

IT ALL FELT SO AMAZINGLY normal. A woman walking with a good looking man and her adorable child through the grocery store, planning cookouts and buying ingredients for s'mores. But it wasn't normal at all. It was a facade that was going to be shattered at any moment. She was sure of it. Her life was going to explode at some point, and the last thing she wanted was for Aaron to get shrapnel all over him.

She watched him with Tyler, and they seemed like father and son already. It was good for Tyler to see a real man. A good man. A loving man. He carried her son on his shoulders just like he was carrying her metaphorically. He was carrying all of them, and she wished it could last forever. She wished that she could erase the past and her fears and her memories. But she couldn't. It was an impossible situation.

They made their way back to the house and settled Tyler into his temporary bedroom which overlooked the pasture behind the house. He was ecstatic to see the ocean off in the distance, and was having a fun time playing with the blocks that Aaron had bought him at the store.

"Make yourself at home," he said to Tessa as he unloaded groceries into the kitchen cabinets and refrigerator. She walked around, touching the thick moldings in the kitchen. "I meant to ask whether you found the makeup mirror you needed?"

"Huh?"

"The makeup mirror? At the pawn shop back there?" He cocked his head at her like she was crazy.

"Oh. No. They didn't have what I needed."

"Is it something I can order for you online?" he asked as he set aside the s'more ingredients on the counter.

"Nah. No big deal. I don't wear much makeup anyway," she said without thinking.

"You certainly don't need it," he said softly as he smiled and looked back down at the three bags of marshmallows on the counter.

"Thanks," she said. He was so nice. She'd never met a man who was so kind. He was the type of guy who'd rescue a turtle from the road or save a ladybug trapped in the window screen. At the same time, he seemed fiercely protective of those he cared about, and she knew that his family came first. She and Tyler weren't his family, and she couldn't cause him to put his mother or the rest of his family in danger by having her around at the wrong time.

No, she'd have to take matters into her own hands. She'd have to do the thing she was most afraid of in the world. When the time was right, she'd have to trust Aaron with her most prized possession and trust herself with her own life.

≈

THE NIGHT AIR was crisp and cool, and Aaron built the bonfire right by the springs. After setting up chairs, he brought Tyler and Tessa outside. Both of them looked like it was the first time they'd seen a fire. Amazement glazed across their faces, and it made Aaron happy to see them happy.

"Wow!" Tyler said jumping up and down.

"Now, listen up, buddy. That fire could really hurt you if you get too close or trip near it, okay? You gotta stay back behind this line," Aaron said drawing a line in the sand with his foot.

Tyler nodded, and Aaron started setting up his skewer with a marshmallow. "We'll do s'mores in a minute, but let's start going through some of these marshmallows your mother bought."

"Hey!" Tessa said laughing as she smacked Aaron on the back. It stung a little, but he kind of liked it.

For the next hour, they chatted and laughed and ate more marshmallows than Aaron had eaten during his whole life combined. He showed Tyler how to make a s'more, and the kid became a wizard at it within half an hour. He showed him how to catch a lightning bug and explained how the ocean tides work.

Aaron felt like a one man show aimed at one goal - teach Tyler everything he could. He was desperately trying to catch Tyler up on all of the things he'd missed in his short life so far.

Still, after an hour, Tyler was tuckered out. He curled up in one of the folding chairs with a blanket around him. A few minutes later, he was out like a light.

"You think he's warm enough?" Tessa asked standing over her son.

"Yeah. That blanket is pretty warm," Aaron said as he stoked the bonfire. "Come sit down," he said patting the seat beside him. He'd dragged an old two-person swing up next to the fire.

Tessa sat down and let out a little sigh as she smiled at him.

"What?" he asked nudging her with his shoulder.

"How did I get so lucky?" she asked softly.

"Lucky?"

"Yes. I must be the luckiest woman alive right now." She shook her head and laughed.

"Seriously? After what you've been through?"

"I'm not talking about that. I'm talking about you, Aaron. What a blessing you've been the past few days." She reached over and took his hand. "Seriously. Thank you."

"You don't have to thank me, Tessa," he said softly.

"I do. You're making Tyler happier than I've ever seen him. He'll never forget this night. You're going to make a great Dad one day. Some woman will be lucky to have you as the father of her children."

"Well, now, that's the nicest thing anyone has ever said to me, Tessa." Inside, he could hear his inner voice shouting that she should be that woman, but he tried to stifle it.

"No matter what happens, I just want you to know how thankful I am."

"No matter what happens? Why are you talking like that, Tessa?" He had a feeling in the pit of his stomach that told him something was wrong. She was acting strangely, and it seemed to have started after they picked Tyler up from his mother's house.

"Do you have any wine?" she asked out of the blue.

"Wine?"

"I haven't had a glass of wine in three years," she said with a smile.

"Then a glass of wine you shall have," he said touching the end of her nose with his finger as he got up and trotted into the house.

~

CRISIS AVERTED, at least for now. She couldn't believe she'd said something so stupid right in front of him. Here he was helping her and her son, and she was making such questionable statements. She would do better, she decided.

"This is so good," she said holding onto the glass of wine like it was the most precious thing on Earth.

"Glad you like it. It's just grocery store wine, but it'll do in a pinch," Aaron said. She stole a glance at him between sips. He was amazingly beautiful for a man, but strong and rugged at the same time. He was staring at the stars above them, a blanket of silver and black across the endless sky.

With his blond hair and striking blue eyes, Aaron Parker was fun to look at. The wine was sinking in a little too much because Tessa's thoughts were getting dirtier than she would've liked. Then she noticed a tattoo on his left arm for the first time. It was on his bicep and said "Never Forgotten".

"Is that for your Dad?" she asked.

"Yeah. I got it when I was seventeen, much to my mother's dismay," he said with a wink. "Adele Parker is not fond of tattoos, but I wanted to honor my Dad in some way."

"I think it's cool," she said running her fingers across it without thinking. The wine was lowering her inhibitions, and she didn't care that she was touching him. He froze for a moment and looked at her, but she continued to touch the tattoo.

And that's when it happened. He reached out and took her hand, pulling her gently to him. She slid across the swing, turning slightly toward him.

"Remember I said that I don't take things without asking?" he whispered. She nodded, and she was sure he could hear her heart pounding. He turned to face her.

"Yes," she said, the air sucked from her lungs.

"I am asking you right now if I can kiss you, Tessa. But it's okay if you say no…" he was saying before she suddenly leaned forward and brushed her lips across his. She could feel his warm breath and smell the scent of grocery store wine, and her pulse quickened.

"Tessa," he growled as he placed his hands on both sides of her face. Holding her there, he pulled back and looked at her. "Are you sure you're okay with this?" he asked, his blue eyes darkened by a mixture of lust and concern. She nodded frantically, desperate for him to cover her mouth with his. And then he did. His full lips began their work, their tongues dancing together as she struggled to regain her breath. Years of loneliness started to wash away. Both of them were wild, uninhibited and like two people who hadn't kissed anyone in years. In reality, she had never kissed anyone like this. With this passion. With this emotion.

"Mommy…" The kiss was broken when Tyler started to stir. Luckily, he hadn't seen them in the throes of passion, but he needed to be put into his bed and get out of the night air.

"I, um… I need to put him…" she stammered, unsure of what to say as she stood up and ceased making eye contact. Why had she allowed herself to get carried away? This was just going to make everything harder for both of them.

"Let me. I'll be back," Aaron said standing up as he walked to Tyler and scooped him up into his strong arms. She looked briefly at his tattoo and remembered how this whole thing had started.

"Aaron, I think it's best if I head to bed too. It's been a long day…" she said, picking up her wine glass and the blanket.

He looked confused, but nodded and then carried Tyler inside. As soon as Tyler was sufficiently tucked in, Tessa kissed his sleeping face goodnight and walked into the darkened hallway.

"Good night," she said softly to Aaron as she opened the door to her room which was across from Tyler's.

"Good night," he said as he leaned against the wall with his hands in his jean pockets. Tessa turned to walk into her room. "Oh, and Tessa?"

"Yes?"

"I had every intention of telling you I was sorry for what happened out there, but I can't. Because I'm not sorry," he said before he turned and walked down the hall. She sucked in a big breath and fought telling him that she wasn't sorry either.

CHAPTER 9

*K*issing Tessa had just made it harder to live in the same house with her. Aaron woke up the next morning and started the day with another cold shower, just like the one he'd had before bed.

He'd never experienced a kiss like that one. In all of the years of what he thought were passionate kisses from Natalie, he'd never felt what he was feeling now - even hours later.

The emotions between them had been creeping up since they'd met. Truth be told, he would've kissed her with the wet dog jumping on him in the rain a few days ago. But it wasn't the mechanics of the kiss. It was the emotion behind it. Like she'd never been kissed before in her life. Like she was starving for water and he was a canteen full of it.

And then she'd pulled back. Stopped. Regret plastered across her face.

He threw on some khaki shorts and a red T-shirt

and headed downstairs to the kitchen. It was still early, and the sun had just come up. He fully expected that Tessa was still asleep, secure in the fact that she was safe in the house with him. But there she stood, already in the kitchen preparing breakfast.

The smell of bacon overwhelmed his senses, and he watched her secretly for a few moments. She moved around the kitchen gracefully, like she'd always done it when he knew she hadn't. She'd never had the chance to be a normal mommy, making PB&J sandwiches and baking cookies at Christmas.

"Have you started the coffee?" he said, causing her to jump and drop the egg she was holding in her hand.

"Oh, gosh, I'm sorry I startled you," Aaron said rushing to her side and grabbing a hand full of paper towels. He crouched to the floor and started cleaning up the mess.

"It's okay, Aaron. You don't have to walk on…"

"Egg shells?" he finished her sentence and then they both started laughing. "Kind of ironic, huh?"

She sat on the floor beside him as he cleaned up the egg mess and she picked out the pieces of shell. Then, their hands collided for a moment and time stood still.

"What is that?" she finally asked softly.

"What is what?" he said without looking up at her for fear of scaring her off again.

"That feeling I get when you touch me."

Aaron sat back against a cabinet and threw the egg covered paper towel into the trashcan behind him. He ran his fingers through his hair, trying desperately not to drag her across the kitchen floor and into his lap.

"You get a feeling?" he asked, trying to sound innocent.

"And you don't?" she asked with a crooked smile.

"Of course not. I find you repulsive," he said tossing a piece of stray egg shell at her. "You're mean and ugly and a terrible kisser, Tessa Reeves."

She crawled across the floor until she was on her knees in front of him and then pelted him with a wadded up paper towel. "Not funny!"

"You're going to give me salmonella!" he said wiping the egg from the paper towel off his face. Both of them were laughing, albeit low to keep from waking Tyler.

"It was a serious question, Aaron. Do you get a feeling?"

"I think it was pretty obvious that I got some feelings about you when we kissed last night, Tessa. And if you'd come to my room after that little episode, you'd have seen some of those feelings visibly, if you know what I mean." A naughty grin crept across his face as hers turned red.

"Aaron!" she said slapping playfully at his leg. "Seriously, I'm sorry about how I reacted. I was up all night thinking about it."

"I was up all night too. Took a cold shower..." he said.

"Very funny."

"Not a joke."

"Really?" she asked with her hand over her mouth.

"Why does that surprise you? You understand male anatomy, don't you?"

"Yes, of course. But... over me?" She seemed amazed that a man would be so attracted to her that he needed a cold shower. It made him sad how little she thought of herself.

"Let me put it this way, Tessa. I've never felt like that in my life. Sure, I've been turned on, aroused, whatever you want to call it. I'm a man. But I've never felt so tied in knots after a kiss in my life. And truthfully, if I never get to experience that again with you, I'll go to my grave feeling like I was screwed out of something special."

Her eyes filled up with tears for a moment, but she took a deep breath and blinked them back. He sat there, looking at her and not speaking. He wasn't sorry he said it, not at all. But he didn't want to push her too hard, too fast.

"You say the sweetest things."

"I'm not being sweet. I'm being honest. I dated Natalie for three freaking years, and I feel like I know you better. I feel like our souls connect, Tessa, and I don't know what to do about it."

"But we can't do this, Aaron." There, she'd said it. And he felt like a dagger had just been driven through his heart. His worst fears confirmed, he sighed and put his head back against the cabinet.

"And why is that?"

"Because I'm no good for you. This whole situation is just you being a good guy and me being a taker. I'm taking your time and your safety from you right now. Even your mother sees it..." She stopped herself and he sat up, stunned.

"What did you just say?" he said a little too loudly as she put her finger over her lips to tell him to quiet down. "My mother? What did she say?"

"Damn it. I didn't mean to say that."

"Tell me what she said, Tessa," he whispered.

"She figured out that I wasn't Dawn. I confessed my name to her, and she guessed that I was running from someone. She was so sweet about it, Aaron, but she made it clear that she just had a stroke and is worried that I'm putting you in danger. I can't do that to you or to her."

His stomach was in knots. His mother was right about one thing. She didn't need the stress of worrying about him getting hurt or killed. Bringing her into the whole thing was a mistake on his part, and now Tessa felt responsible. What a mess.

"I'll talk to her," he said softly.

"There's nothing to say, Aaron. She's right. She's your mother, and I would feel the same way if Tyler had put himself in the position you're in right now. Until the threat of Ethan is neutralized, anyone around me is in danger, including my son. I don't intend to add you and your mother to that mix."

"I need to call her and explain that he's being watched so she can at least have some peace for now. I wish you'd told me this last night."

"I know. I should have. I just didn't know what to say." She looked down, and he hated the sadness in her eyes.

"Tessa?"

"Yeah?"

"Does this mean we can't kiss anymore?" he asked with a chuckle to break the ice. She smiled sadly and then stood up. He followed her.

"It was amazing, Aaron. And, for the record, I've never felt that way before either. I wish we were in a different situation, but we aren't."

"I won't push you. I promise. If that's the only kiss I ever get from you, I will hold it right here for the rest of my life," he said touching his chest. She reached out and put her hand on his and then brought his hand to her heart area.

"Me too," she said softly as a stray tear rolled down her cheek. And then they heard Tyler coming down the stairs, and the moment was over.

≈

FOR THE NEXT THREE DAYS, Aaron did exactly what he'd promised at the outset of their trip. He was teaching Tyler everything he knew about the outdoors.

He took him out in the canoe and attempted teaching him to row, but they almost toppled over and Tessa made him stop. Then, he'd taught him to fish, catch turtles and make the world's best sandcastles along the shore of the springs.

In between, he'd shown him how to make paper airplanes and build castles out of blocks. It was like watching a dying father show his child everything he could before taking his final breath. Aaron was leaving nothing unsaid or undone when it came to Tyler, and

Tessa wondered if he thought she would take off with her son without telling him.

It made Tessa's heart ache every time she watched Aaron show her son how to do something. She thought about how much Tyler had missed in his young life by not having a real father. And yet here she was having to push away a man who obviously wanted to spend time with her and her son. Ethan was still pulling the strings even without trying, and the thought of it made her sick to her stomach.

How did she get here? She never expected to meet a man that she could see herself falling in love with, but here he was. She watched him outside as he played catch with Tyler and wondered how she could get herself out of the situation. She would never be able to go on with her life knowing that a man like Aaron was out there and would have stood by her through thick and thin.

Sure, a part of her didn't want to trust him after everything that had happened with Ethan, but her heart knew that Aaron was a good person who would take care of her and Tyler if she would only allow him to.

She had to do something. She'd been mulling over her plans in her mind for the last couple days, and there seemed to be no other option. She had to take a stand and be courageous if she had wanted any chance of being with Aaron when all was said and done.

$\sim$

As EVENING FELL, Tyler was exhausted and fell asleep on the sofa. They'd had a large dinner, and Tessa was finally starting to relax. The old house was becoming home after only four days, and that scared her a little bit. Even Beau was enjoying the springs and having so much room to run around outside.

"Boy, he's out like a light," Aaron said as he turned off the kitchen light and walked into the living room.

"Yeah. This is more activity than he's had in his whole life," Tessa said with a laugh.

"Want some wine? It's beautiful out there tonight. We could sit on the deck and enjoy the quiet," he said with a wink, insinuating that little Tyler was energetic and loud.

"That sounds perfect."

They covered Tyler with a blanket and walked onto the deck. Aaron poured them each a glass of wine as they sat down on the log hewn Adirondack chairs flanking the back deck.

"To new beginnings," he said softly as he held up his wine glass.

"New beginnings," she repeated as their glasses clinked together. "So, have you heard from Stan today?"

"No. Not today. But I expect to hear from him anytime now."

"Why would you say that?" she asked, her stomach a pit of nervous knots and what felt like angry butterflies.

"Well, given what you told me about your ex, I assume he's concocting a plan. Don't you think so?"

"Yes. Of course. I have to wonder, though…"

"What?"

"I'm just wondering if I should keep waiting for him to come after me, or if I…"

"If you what? Go after him? Are you crazy?" Aaron said with a little more anger in his voice than she would have liked.

"Not exactly…"

"Tessa, listen to me. This man is no one you want to play around with. You have to promise me that you won't do anything stupid like confront him. Promise me," he said with a look of seriousness in his eyes that she hadn't seen previously.

"I promise," she said softly. "But it's nice to know you care so much."

"You know I care, Tessa. Too much." Her heart felt like it was going to jump right out of her chest at his words. She hated that she was going to break the promise she'd just made, but she felt like it was her only way out. It was her ticket to freedom. It was her one shot lottery ticket that she hoped would pay off and not end in her funeral.

"How about some music?" she said changing the subject to quiet her mind.

"Sure. I've got my phone in my pocket," he said as he fumbled with the wine glass. A moment later, he had the music going.

"I love this song," she said as "The Way You Look Tonight" started to play. Aaron put his glass on the table and stood, holding his hand out to her. She cocked her head at him.

"May I have this dance?" he asked softly. Again, her heart skipped so many beats that she feared she might pass out. She nodded and stood as he pulled her out into the open area of the deck.

They stood facing each other for a moment before he slipped his hands around her waist and slowly pulled her closer. Heat radiated throughout her body as she struggled to keep air in her lungs. Sliding her hands up his arms, she settled them on his strong shoulders and stared at his chest. Unable to look up at him, she continued staring straight ahead and holding her breath.

"Tessa, look at me," he whispered into her ear, sending shivers down her neck as his nose brushed against her skin.

She tilted her head up slightly and allowed her eyes to lock in on his. Swallowing hard, she fell in step with the rhythm of the music and realized what a good dancer he was. He held her strong and confidently, and she felt safe in his arms.

Her lips were getting dry, so she ran her tongue across her bottom lip. He sighed and looked up for a moment before looking back down at her with a wry smile.

"What?" she whispered.

"You're killing me."

"Why?"

"Stop licking your lips. Please."

"I didn't know I was licking my lips," she lied.

"I think you know exactly what you're doing, Tessa Reeves," he said pulling her closer. "And if you don't stop, I might just die right here in this spot. And you'll have to clean up an Aaron sized puddle right here." He stomped his foot lightly as she giggled.

She tightened her grip around his neck and put her head on his chest, which generated yet another sigh from him. Looking up, she said, "I'm sorry. Is it not okay if I put my head on your chest?"

"Tessa, you can put your head anywhere on my body that you want to," he responded which generated a small slap from her.

"Aaron!" she said with a laugh. "You're bad."

"You have no idea."

"Maybe you've had too much wine," she said before noticing that his glass was still full and sitting on the table.

"No, I've had enough of being near a woman that I find to be immensely attractive and perfect for me but not being able to touch her or hold her or kiss her. I've had enough of some jackass rogue cop ruling our lives from another state. I've had enough of rubbing against you on this deck and not being able to press my lips to yours and wash away all of your fears for just a moment. That's what I've had enough of." He wasn't laughing, and Tessa knew he was dead serious.

"Aaron…"

"No, listen to me, Tessa. My mother will be okay. She's a strong woman who loves me, and I could tell she really liked you. And she's going to worry no matter what I do. What I know for sure is that you were put in my life for a reason, and I'm not going to take a chance of losing the opportunity we could have to be together. What I need to know is whether you feel the same. Do you have feelings for me? I mean, would you be interested in seeing where this goes?"

She stopped swaying and broke their embrace, although he kept his hands on her waist.

"I'm sorry. I pushed too hard. I'm sorry," he repeated. She just stood there, like an idiot, and stared straight ahead. "Tessa?"

Her heart was skipping and those dang butterflies were whirling around in her stomach. She wanted to speak, but her mouth wouldn't cooperate with her. She wanted to say yes, she had strong feelings for him. She wanted to say yes, please save me from myself and my fears. She wanted to say yes. Yes. Yes... But, she couldn't say anything.

Realizing that she wasn't able to speak, Aaron pulled her back in again and started swaying to the music. He knew just what to do, but she was angry with herself. How could she let him say those things to her and then not respond? It wasn't right.

"Aaron," she whispered against his chest, tears rolling down her cheeks.

"Yes?" he whispered back, continuing to sway.

"I feel the same way too."

"Good," he said giving her a squeeze. "Then everything is going to work out. You just wait and see."

CHAPTER 10

*T*t was three in the morning when she heard the sound of someone talking. Grabbing a heavy vase from her nightstand, Tessa crept up the hallway toward the voice. That's when she realized it was Aaron talking on the phone as softly as he could out on his private deck.

It wasn't his fault that his voice woke her up. Over the years of living with Ethan, she'd trained herself to wake up to every little sound just in case he was coming to abuse her or kidnap Tyler. She was sure that she could hear a leaf blowing across the yard even if she was in a dead sleep.

Knowing it was wrong, she walked closer so she could hear Aaron talking. He was definitely whispering so that she couldn't hear him.

"Listen, Stan, I need to know where he's headed… You think the campground? Well, how long has he been on the road?"

Oh, God. Ethan was on the move. She'd have to

move her plan up quite a bit to make sure that she had time.

"He left an hour ago? That doesn't give me much time. No, we aren't there, but it's only a matter of time. No, I can't wake her up. That'll scare her to death. I'll just wait until morning and then break the news to her. We'll stay locked down here, so keep your guy on him. Once he gets to the campground, tell your guy to back off. I don't want him to know he's being followed, okay?"

That was perfect. She wanted the private investigator to back off so Ethan entered the campground alone. Tessa sneaked back into her room and quickly changed her clothes, preparing herself for the scariest thing she would ever do in her life.

~

AARON COULDN'T SLEEP after his phone call with Stan. He was wracking his brain about how to best protect Tessa and Tyler, and the weight of the problem was giving him the worst case of insomnia he'd ever had.

If he reported the situation to local police, they would just have to give it to Ethan's department. And she had no proof. Without proof, she had nothing. And what if Ethan tried to fight for custody of Tyler? That just couldn't happen, Aaron thought. He'd hide them forever if he had to.

Pacing his room, he decided that a strong cup of coffee was in order. Maybe Tessa was up too, although he hoped she was getting some sleep. She didn't know

Ethan was on his way to find her. She needed a few more hours of peace because the onslaught was coming.

He crept up the hallway, but noticed Tessa's door was cracked open. Unable to keep from seeing how she looked while she was peacefully sleeping, he peeked in. The room was dark, of course, but the light of the moon was streaming in the window and bathing the bed in a sea of muted shades of blue. But he didn't see a lump in the bed. He didn't see Tessa.

Willing to risk her getting mad, he flipped on the light switch. She wasn't in the bed. "Tessa?" he whispered as he walked around the room. She wasn't in her adjoining bathroom either.

As he started to run out the door, worried that she'd fallen down the winding staircase, he saw a piece of paper on her dresser. It was a letter to him, and its contents took his breath away.

Dear Aaron,

Wow. Where do I begin? You've been such a godsend for me and Tyler these last few days, and I can't believe the feelings I've developed for you in such a short time. I thought I'd never feel that way about anyone, but there you were.

And then it dawned on me that I will never be free until Ethan isn't. I can't go on living like a fugitive. I want to grab everything that life has to offer me, and I want Tyler to have the best life possible. So, I had to make a decision.

Tyler is still sleeping soundly in his bed, and I pray that you will watch over him until I get back. I'm sorry to put such responsibility on you, but I couldn't put him in more danger. This is my problem to deal with, and it's time to stand up and fight.

And, God forbid, if something happens to me, please take care of my son. He doesn't have anyone else, and he adores you.

Until we meet again,

Tessa

Aaron's heart was pounding as he tried to think through what she was doing. He had to get to her before it was too late. But why did she leave in the middle of the night like that? What prompted her…

Wait, he thought. She must have heard him on the phone. That was about an hour ago, so he still had time to get to her.

Aaron made a call to his brother, Kyle, and asked him to come babysit Tyler for awhile. He told Kyle that he had an emergency come up at the campground, but he knew that Kyle didn't buy it.

After he arrived, Aaron told him what to say to Tyler when he woke up and headed outside to his car. Tessa didn't take the car, obviously, so he wasn't sure how she got anywhere on foot. It would take her over an hour to walk to the campground, and it would be dangerous for her to do. Then it dawned on him. The bicycle he normally kept on the porch was gone.

"Oh, God," he muttered to himself as he started the car. "Why do women have to be so stubborn?"

He peeled down the driveway as fast as he could, hoping against hope that he would somehow get to Tessa before Ethan did.

~

Tessa's legs were aching tired when she pulled into the campground on the rickety old bicycle that was on Aaron's porch. She had no idea how old the thing was, but it wasn't nearly as state of the art as she'd hoped when she left.

Her hope was that Aaron was fast asleep and wouldn't know what she'd done until morning. She prayed that he wouldn't hate her, and that Tyler was safe with him.

The funny thing was that her adrenaline was pumping so much from the bike ride that she was no longer scared. She was ready to fight for her freedom no matter what happened.

She pulled the old bike behind her dilapidated camper and walked up to the door. Ethan's car was nowhere to be seen and the campground was eerily quiet with only the sound of the waves off in the distance.

Her plan was to sit in the camper, hot as it was, and wait for Ethan to arrive. As she unlocked the door, something just didn't feel right but before she could figure out what it was, Ethan's strong arm came out from the darkness of the camper and pulled her inside violently.

She didn't have time to scream as he put his other hand over her mouth and dragged her to the floor, kicking the door shut behind her.

Writhing around, trying to wiggle away from him, she kicked randomly in the air. He picked her up and threw her across the room, and she landed on the floor with a thud just beside the bedroom door.

Backing up, she stood and leaned against the wall, hands in her pockets.

"You stupid bitch. Did you really think you could run from me? Get your hands out of your pockets."

"Ethan, now listen…" she said, begging him to relax as she held up her hands. It never worked, but she needed to buy some time and calm him down. She was sure he had a gun on him somewhere. He always did.

"You ran from me while my father was sick? What kind of person does that?" he said, surprising her with his level of emotion.

"Ethan, you were holding me hostage. For three years. And our son…"

"Where is he? Where's my kid?" he said, suddenly looking around angrily.

"He's somewhere safe. It was too hot in here…"

"I bet you've been whoring around already!" he yelled walking closer to her.

"Why did you do it?" she suddenly asked, breaking his chain of thought.

"Do what?" he asked staring into her eyes with more anger than she'd ever seen from him. She stared back, which only seemed to anger him more. She'd never stood up to him. Never asked questions.

"Why did you hold me hostage for three long years, Ethan? Why couldn't you just love me like a normal man?"

"You know why."

"Tell me, Ethan. Tell me so we can work this out. I

want to come home. I want to make things right," she said softly, the words causing vomit to rise up in her throat. If this was going to work, she had to make him believe that she wanted him back.

"Do I look like a fool? I'm not falling for this little ploy, Tessa. I'm a frigging cop. Don't you think I see through your little charade?" he said as he stalked closer and closer to her.

"Fine, I don't want you back. You're a worthless bastard who held me hostage for three years, and I hope you rot in hell for all of the abuse you did to me," she said, rage seething through her gritted teeth. If sweetness wasn't working, she made a last minute decision to see if rage would. She was angry, and if the last thing she did on Earth was blast him with her words, it would be worth it.

"You deserved it. You aren't worth shit, Tessa. You never were, and you never will be. And now, because you've tried to humiliate me, you're going to pay the ultimate price," he pulled a gun from his pocket and pointed it at her head. "And you know what, not a damn soul on this Earth will give a shit that you're gone. That kid of yours will be mine, and I'll make sure to find him a nice home."

"He's your son. How can you say that?" she said through her still gritted teeth as she eyed the gun.

"I'm a bastard, you said so yourself. I never wanted a kid, but you still managed to get yourself knocked up, didn't you? And who knows if I'm even the father of him. You were such a slut."

His alcohol laced breath washed over her face and made her want to throw up.

"I never cheated on you, Ethan, and you know it," she said softly as she slid her hand into her pocket slowly.

"You flirted with every man in town, Tessa. And that guy on Facebook…"

"Damn, Ethan, I've told you a hundred times that I never cheated on you," she said, tears starting to well up in her eyes as she realized the gun was still pointing at her head and he was getting angrier.

"Stop playing me for a fool!" he yelled as he hit her in the side of the head with the gun. Pain shot through her eyes, and she struggled to stay upright.

There was no more time to wait. Her life was about to end, and she had to make one more last ditch effort to save herself and Tyler. With every bit of power she had in her petite body, she kneed Ethan in the groin. The surprise of it caused him to bend forward and drop the gun below her head. It was only for a moment, but it was long enough for her to pull out the knife she'd bought at the pawn shop and stab him straight in the stomach with it.

Tessa didn't wait to see the outcome. Instead, she ran straight out of the camper into the darkened woods screaming for help. And that's when she turned to see Ethan coming out of the camper and headed toward her.

∾

Aaron drove as fast as he could and skidded into the campground. He had a bad feeling, but he hoped he was wrong. As he pulled into the driveway next to his cabin, he jumped out looking for the bicycle. It was leaned against the back of Tessa's camper, so he jogged across the yard. Before he could make it there, he heard a gunshot and his heart sank.

"Tessa?" he screamed as he ran into the woods behind her camper. He couldn't see anything in the darkness of the early morning hours. "Tessa? Please, answer me!" he yelled.

"Aaron?" he heard her answer softly. He pulled out his cell phone and turned on his flashlight app.

Tessa was sitting on the ground behind a tree, shaking in fear and crying. Her eyes were glassy and staring straight ahead.

"Tessa? What happened, honey? Where is he?"

"There," she said shakily as she pointed to a lifeless body on the ground about ten feet away.

"You killed him? How did you get a gun?"

"I don't have a gun. I didn't shoot him. I stabbed him in the camper, but he followed me out here..."

"Then who shot him?" Aaron asked.

"I did," a male voice said in the darkness. As he walked closer, Aaron realized it was Paul, his right hand man.

"Paul?" Aaron asked incredulously. "But how did you..."

"I was coming home from a date and saw her running. The guy was pointing a gun. You know I always carry mine with me..."

"Thank God you do, man," Aaron said, standing up and shaking Paul's hand. "You saved a life today."

"And I took one," he said looking down. "I didn't mean to kill him, Aaron. I was trying to shoot his leg, but I couldn't see well."

"How do you know he's... dead?" Tessa asked softly.

"I checked for a pulse. I'm a part-time EMT. There was no pulse. No signs of life," Paul said. "This guy, he was the one you were hiding from, right?"

"Yes," she whispered, still looking straight ahead. The sun was starting to peek up over the horizon now, yet she still sat shaking on the ground.

"Did you call the police?" Aaron asked Paul.

"Yeah. They should be here any minute," he said.

"Thank you," Tessa said softly as she finally looked up at Paul. "You really did save my life. He had a gun to my head in there, and he was going to kill me."

"I'm glad I could help you. Dawn, right? Or Dana?" he asked.

"Actually, my name is Tessa Reeves. And I'm free now," she said, a haunting tone in her voice.

~

THE POLICE CAME moments later and took both Tessa and Paul into Aaron's cabin for questioning. Aaron sat nervously outside, worried that his friend or the woman he was falling in love with might be taken to jail. Finally, Tessa and Paul appeared outside and the officer drove off in his car.

"Well?" Aaron said.

"That was difficult," she said softly as he put his hands on her shoulders and rubbed them up and down. "But I had the evidence I needed."

"Evidence? I thought you didn't have anything?"

"The day I went into the pawn shop, I sold the one thing I had left. It was my grandmother's wedding ring. I swore I'd never sell it, but I knew that was the only way I would ever get out of this mess. So, I got a little cash and a digital audio recorder from the pawn shop. I also bought a knife. My plan was to put gas in the camper and drive back to confront him so that I could record our conversation, only I heard you on the phone with Stan early this morning…"

"Tessa, are you crazy? Why didn't you tell me? Let me help you? I don't understand…" Aaron was more than a little upset. He was hurt and offended that in the end she didn't seem to trust him.

"I needed to do it on my own, Aaron. I've had to depend on a man for everything for my entire life. And those men let me down. I needed to know I was capable of being brave and strong for myself. I can't depend on you for everything," she said, tears streaming down her face. "Anyway, I taped everything he said to me. The recorder even kept going during our struggle. It was an obvious case of self defense, so the police aren't going to bring charges."

"Guys, I'm gonna go and let y'all talk, okay?" Paul could sense the tension in the air.

"Man, I don't know how to thank you," Aaron said putting his hand on Paul's shoulder and shaking his hand with the other.

"No need to thank me. I just did what I thought needed to be done in the heat of the moment."

"Let me know if you need anything. Time off…"

"No, I think I need to work. Keep my mind off this stuff for awhile," he said. "Gotta go try to get some sleep." With that, Paul walked up the pathway toward his own cabin.

Tessa was now staring out over the ocean in the distance, her hands pressed against the railing. She was somewhere else in her mind, as if she was trying to escape her current situation.

"Oh, God, where is Tyler?" she said suddenly, looking around.

"He's okay. My brother, Kyle, took him home to play with Kaitlyn today. He just thinks it's a play date," Aaron said softly, putting his arms around her and pulling her close. He could hear her sniffing and then she broke into uncontrollable sobs, her body jolting over and over again from the pain of it all. The walls were crumbling down, and it was a violent thing to witness. Still, when he thought about what could have happened if Paul hadn't been coming home just at the right time, it made him feel ill.

"I can't believe he's dead. After everything he did to me, I still didn't want him dead. You have to believe me," she sobbed.

"Oh, Tessa, I know that. You're a good person. You'd never wish someone dead. He made those decisions, and it led where it led. It's not your fault."

"I don't know what to do now," she said softly. "I've

lived in fear for so long, I don't think I know how to be free."

"We'll figure it out together, Tessa," he said hugging her tighter. She pulled back and looked up at him.

"I don't think I can do that." His heart felt like it stopped for a moment.

"What?"

"There's a part of me that says I need to be here with you, wrapped up in the comfort of your arms. Then there's another part of me that says I need to see if I can make it on my own."

"You want to be alone?" he asked, cocking his head to the side in confusion.

"I don't want to be. I think I have to be. I need to find out who I really am. What I'm made of. What kind of mother I can be on my own. I went from my father's house to Ethan's house, and I've never been on my own. I've never gotten to see what accomplishment or independence feels like. I just sat there in that camper, watching my life pass before my eyes, and realized that there isn't much to look back on and be proud of."

Aaron ran his fingers through his hair, a sure sign of being stressed out, and groaned.

"I'm not going to beg you to stay, Tessa. You're a grown woman. I have no question what you're made of, but apparently you do. I want you here. I want *you*. Can you see that?" he asked looking into her eyes.

"I want you too, but I need to do this, Aaron. I need a new start. I need to make sure I'm at one hundred percent before I give my heart away again."

"Are you sure you're clear headed enough to make

such an important decision right now, Tessa? You're tired..."

"No! This isn't about being tired. I know what I need to do for myself, and if you can't understand that then I'm sorry. I appreciate all of your help, Aaron. Now please take me back to my son, okay?" she said turning away from him. The wall went back up, and Aaron decided he was tired of trying to tear it down.

CHAPTER 11

*I*t was her final day in January Cove, and Tessa's stomach was in knots. She'd spent the last few days talking with police, avoiding phone calls from Ethan's family and looking for a new place to live in Savannah.

She'd already secured a job at a marketing company in Savannah, just to get her by until she could get on her feet. She'd found the perfect little one bedroom apartment for her and Tyler right in downtown Savannah. But one thing she hadn't been able to do yet was say goodbye to Aaron.

He'd spent a lot of time with Tyler while she was packing up. Several people around town heard her story and actually chipped in to buy her a used car, and that had made her cry. She sold off the awful camper to get enough money to put a deposit on her apartment, but her job would be their only source of income so she had to make it work.

Adele Parker had come to say goodbye and tell her

how proud she was of the strength Tessa showed. It meant a lot to her, and she'd cried at that too. On her last day, Kyle and Jenna came by so she finally got a chance to meet them. Jenna took her aside.

"Tessa, I know we just met, but I see a lot of myself in you," she'd said. "And I kind of understand why you're doing this. But let me tell you something I know for sure. These Parker men, they get under your skin. It's an itch you'll never be able to scratch with anyone else," she said with a smile. "I hope you don't take too long finding yourself because that Aaron is a gem, honey. You'd be one lucky woman to land him." Tessa gave her a hug and nodded.

"Thanks. And I know you're right. I just... have to do this. For me."

When it was time for her to leave, it was just her and Aaron and Tyler. Like a little family, she thought, and then shook the idea from her head.

She packed her last bag into the small compact car as Aaron stood in the driveway of the cabin. Tyler ran to him and gave him a big hug.

"Bye, buddy. I'll see you soon, I promise. Maybe we can see a movie or something in a few weeks," Aaron said ruffling Tyler's hair.

"I wish we didn't have to go. I like it here."

"I know, but sometimes adults have to do things even when they don't make a lick of sense at all," Aaron said looking up at Tessa, his mouth forming a sharp line.

He gave Tyler another squeeze before he got into

the car and buckled up. Tessa stood there and looked at Aaron.

"I'm sorry," she said softly.

"Goodbye, Tessa," he said holding his hand up and forcing a smile. "And good luck. I hope you find what you're looking for." With that, he turned and walked inside. And Tessa's heart felt like it actually broke in two.

~

Two Months Later

"Over to the left more," Aaron said to Gary, his favorite contractor. "Perfect."

He'd spent the last four weeks renovating the house by the springs, and the finishing touches were going into the kitchen with new cabinets.

"Those are nice cabinets," Gary said. "You must have paid a pretty penny for those."

"Yeah. I ordered them directly from the cabinet maker so they would fit in with the time period of the house. I want it to look authentic."

"When does the bed and breakfast open anyway?" Gary asked as he took a long gulp of water.

"Not for another few weeks yet. I wanted some time here alone before I start that up. Plus, I have to find someone to run the place. I'm busy at the campground a lot."

"Then why did you decide to do this now?"

"I just needed to. The place needs energy, and it has some good memories for me."

Aaron got lost in his thoughts for a moment as he remembered those good times with Tessa and Tyler. Tipping over in the canoe. Making s'mores by the campfire. Kissing in the swing. He'd gone over and over those memories in his mind since she left. His heart still ached for her just the same, and he dreamed of her most nights. She'd only called once, and that was to let Tyler talk to him. He missed the boy almost as much as he missed Tessa, but he was well aware that she wanted space and independence and he was going to give it to her.

As Gary went back to his work, Aaron walked out to the front yard to get something from his car. When he made it to the front porch, he was shocked to see someone standing there. Natalie.

"What in God's name are you doing here?" he said shaking his head.

"Heard you were finally renovating this old place."

"You heard right. But that still doesn't explain why you're here." He walked past her to his car, took out his phone and shut the door.

"We need to talk. Or at least I need to talk."

"We most certainly do not need to talk, Natalie. Jeez, it's been six months now. What could we possibly have to talk about?" He started to walk back up the stairs, but she grabbed his arm and turned him around.

"Aaron, I made a huge mistake. I was scared, and I had no idea what I had until it was gone. I want you back. I want a chance to prove that I love you, and I won't ever cheat on you again," she said, tears welling in her lying eyes.

"You have got to be kidding me," he said with a laugh.

"This isn't funny, Aaron. I'm serious. I know you were dating that trailer park woman and she left you after she killed her husband...."

He stared into her eyes, cutting a hole right through her. "Don't you ever talk that way about Tessa. She's more of a woman than you'll ever be. And she didn't murder anyone."

"Still, you have to know that you'd be so much better off with a woman like me, Aaron. Come on, you were seriously slumming it with her." She rolled her eyes, and Aaron did everything he could not to punch a woman.

"Natalie, get off my property. Now." He tried to stay calm, but she was riling him up and he didn't need the extra aggravation of having her removed.

"What, do you want me to beg?" she asked, starting to kneel on the ground.

"Good Lord, get up, woman!" he said yanking her arm which sent her tumbling into his chest. She took that opportunity to lace her arms around his neck and press her lips to his. Natalie was pretty strong for such a thin frame, and he had trouble wrestling away from her grip.

Before he could say anything, a noise beside them caught his attention. He looked over and saw Tessa standing there, but she had dropped her purse on the ground. Her eyes were wide, like she'd seen a ghost, and she shook her head before grabbing her purse and running up the long gravel driveway.

"Tessa!" he yelled, wrenching free of Natalie's grip as Natalie called to him over and over. Eventually, he could no longer hear her voice, but could only hear Tessa's footsteps running faster and faster. She was wearing a sundress and sandals, but she sure was fast. "Wait! Tessa! Please!" he yelled.

Finally, she stopped out of sheer exhaustion and leaned against a tree. Her ragged breaths shuddered in and out as she bent over with her hands on her knees.

"I'm sorry I came," she said.

"I'm not," he said as he knelt on the ground in front of her.

"Who is she?"

"Natalie. My ex."

"You took her back?" she asked with a confused look on her face.

"Of course not. She just showed up out of the blue trying to get me to agree to come back. I was trying to say no, but she kissed me before I could stop her. I didn't want to kiss her, Tessa. I didn't even want to see her."

"I have no right to tell you who to kiss anyway," she said as she finally stood up. Aaron stood with her.

"Why are you here?" he asked softly, hoping for a good answer.

She seemed to be weighing her options as to what to say. "No, I said I was going to be honest and I am," she said to herself. "I'm here because I fell in love with you two months ago, and I left because I thought I had something to prove. What I ended up proving was that being with a man who cares about me doesn't make me weak. It makes me stronger." Her eyes were filled with tears as she bit her bottom lip to stop herself from crying.

"Don't bite your lip. You know what that does to me," he said with a sly smile. "You love me? Really?"

"Yes, really. So much it hurts," she said.

"I love you too, Tessa Reeves. More than I've ever loved anyone. But I can't have you running away from me again. I need you to trust me, and I'll trust you. We've both been hurt and betrayed in different ways, but I am willing to stand in the gap for you. I will always protect you if you'll let me. Can you promise me that you won't ever run off like that again?"

"I promise. It was stupid. I know that now."

They stood there staring at each other for a moment before Aaron stepped forward and placed his hands on both of her cheeks.

"God, I've missed you," he said as he leaned in and kissed her softly. "Everything about you, I've missed. This nose," he said as he kissed her nose, "these cheeks," he said as he brushed her cheek with his lips. "this neck," he said as he planted a series of kisses up her neck. She moaned at his touch and seemed to be losing her legs for a moment. He slowly pushed her back against the tree and covered her mouth with his, pulling her as close to him as possible. Just then, the sound of a car squealing down the driveway interrupted the moment.

"I hate you!" Natalie yelled out the window before throwing a rock at Aaron and driving away.

"Good to see you again, Nat!" he yelled back laughing before he returned to Tessa's lips.

A few moments later, they each pulled back to take a breath. Tessa was all smiles, and Aaron loved to see that side of her.

"Where's Tyler?"

"With your Mom," she said grinning.

"What?"

"Your mother came to see me last week, Aaron. She told me that she thought we belonged together, and that you were lost without me. Is that true?" She twirled a piece of her hair around her finger.

"My meddling mother," he said laughing. "But yes, that is totally true."

"She told me that you were looking to hire someone to run this bed and breakfast, and I wanted to apply for that job. Would you like to see my resume?"

"Oh, I'd love to see your resume. But we will have to conduct this interview in my bedroom." Tessa's eyes got big and her mouth fell open.

"Why, Aaron Parker, I'm going to tell your mama on you!" she said in her best Southern drawl.

"Tessa?"

"Yes?" she said as they started to walk back to the house.

"Where is your car?"

"At the end of the driveway. I ran out of gas," she said giggling.

"Some things never change. Have you ever noticed that every time you run out of gas, you end up where I am? I think that's a sign," he said as he grabbed her up in his arms and started carrying her.

"A sign of what, Mr. Parker?"

"A sign that any road you take will always lead you back to me," he said kissing her gently. She put her head on his chest, content in the fact that Aaron Parker was fully qualified to love her forever.

~

To get a list of Rachel Hanna's books, visit www. RachelHannaAuthor.com.

Made in the USA
Columbia, SC
19 December 2021

52233249R00098